RECEIVED

NO LONGER PROPERTY OF
SEATTLE PUBLIC LIBRARY

Praise for *Love in Infant Monkeys*

"These incredibly crafted stories, with their rare intelligence, humor, and empathy, describe the furious collision of nature and science, man and animal, everyday citizen and celebrity, fact and fiction."   —Joe Meno, author of *Hairstyles of the Damned*

"You could read this collection as a critique—of our celebrity culture, of the uses we make of unresponding creatures—and Millet is sufficiently thorough to layer these resonances in a satisfying way. But that would be to miss the pleasures of the best of these stories: their quickness, their minor graces . . . A story collection too varied to be packaged as a kind of novel is a refreshing thing."
                                                —*The New York Times Book Review*

"With any justice, this collection finally gets Millet recognized as one of the great short-story writers of our time."
                                                —*The Courier-Journal*

"Millet's best work, an expert mix of elegant satire and understated humanity."   —*Quill & Quire*

"Millet comments on our relationship to nature, the way we try so hard to stand outside it when in fact we are at its mercy every moment of our lives."   —*Chicago Tribune*

"At times touches the sublime."   —*Bitch*

"These stories ripple with emotion and insight. Lydia Millet is a writer of remarkable intelligence and ability, one whose work, like the celebrities and animals that populate *Love in Infant Monkeys*, holds a mirror up to the life itself."
                                                —*The Globe and Mail*

D0958567

"The most thought provoking short story collection since Judy Budnitz's *Flying Leap* . . . In seamless prose beset with wit and an overzealous imagination, Lydia Millet has turned out a collection of great wonder and sadness . . . a . . . wild-eyed, book of truth . . . a transformative look into the lives of others and into ourselves."　　　　　　　　　　　　　　　—*Venus Zine*

"Heartbreakingly explore[s] humans' myriad bonds with and psychological uses for animals."　　　　　　—*The Austin Chronicle*

"Millet is the greatest American author of her generation. She breaks rules by turning author polemic into poetry while at the same time allowing the kind of characters most writers wouldn't touch to own the stories outright."　　　—*Eye Weekly* (Toronto)

"Short, startling, terrifically inventive stories . . . funny too, but many manage to be even more than that—beautiful, serious, breathtakingly sad. [Millet's] work takes rare risks with subject matter and form, and does so with a sense of jazzy improvisation . . . all these stories are animated by a playful, unconfined energy that makes them intensely pleasurable to read."　　—*The Rumpus*

"Brilliant and audacious . . . Millet archly plucks famous people out of history books and the tabloids and places them at the nucleus of acerbic yet elegiac tales about stark encounters with other species . . . Millet turns from droll and caustic to haunting and tragic in concise yet psychologically and morally intricate stories."　　　　　　　　　　—*Booklist*, starred review

"Absolutely beautiful stories. Perfect, in their own way, just like the animals they describe. The title piece—*Love in Infant Monkeys*, about the infamous experimental psychologist Harry Harlow—moved me to tears. Others are deeply mysterious. I love the way Millet writes—magnificent."

—Jeffrey Moussaieff Masson, author of *When Elephants Weep*

Praise for HOW THE DEAD DREAM

A *Los Angeles Times* and *Globe and Mail*
Best Book of the Year

"The writing is always flawlessly beautiful, reaching for an experience that precedes language itself." —*Salon*

"Millet's extraordinary leap of a novel warns us that as the splendor and mystery of the natural world is replaced by the human-made, our species faces a lonely and spiritually impoverished future." —*Booklist* (starred review)

"In her novels, abstract, poetic passages bemoan the fate of humanity alongside goofy, broad-stroked depictions . . . [*How the Dead Dream*] is no exception . . . [it] synthesizes the two styles of Millet's fiction—the harrowing and the madcap—with a new elegance." —*San Francisco Chronicle*

"[Millet's] best when she makes startlingly odd events seem wholly real . . . but what's more profound is Millet's understanding of the loneliness and alienation in a world being poisoned to death." —*The Washington Post*

"Millet . . . writes fiction that confronts social issues without falling into shrill hectoring or dull didacticism . . . her steady hand and subtle voice are what make them work as well as they do." —*The Believer*

"[Millet] has pulled off her funniest, most shrewdly thoughtful and touching novel. If Kurt Vonnegut were still alive, he would be extremely jealous." —*Village Voice*

Praise for OH PURE AND RADIANT HEART

A *Booklist* and *Boldtype* Best Book of the Year

"[An] extremely smart . . . resonant fantasy."
—*The New York Times Book Review*

"Millet . . . boldly fuses lyrical realism with precisely rendered far-out-ness to achieve a unique energy and perspicacity, the ideal approach to the most confounding reality of our era: the atomic bomb." —*Booklist* (starred review)

"Lydia Millet is da bomb. Literally . . . Though *Oh Pure and Radiant Heart* possesses the nervy irreverence of Kurt Vonnegut and Joseph Heller, Millet makes the subject matter her own, capturing the essence of these geniuses in a way that can only be described as, well, genius." —*Vanity Fair*

"Brilliant and fearless . . . Millet takes a headlong run at the subject of nuclear annihilation, weaving together black comedy, science, history, and time travel to produce, against stiff odds, a shattering and beautiful work." —*Entertainment Weekly*

"[A] unique and wide-reaching book . . . Its head soars into philosophical inquiry about love and peace and creative ambition; its heart is planted in the emotional and psychological landscape of its characters and those who have been terrorized by the bomb; and its feet are sunk firmly into the political reality of greed, manipulation, and opportunism." —*Bloomsbury Review*

Praise for MY HAPPY LIFE

Winner of the PEN USA Award for Fiction

"A prodigious feat."   —*New York Times Book Review*

"If there were any justice in the world, *My Happy Life* would become not merely a cult book, devoured by a few astonished readers every year, but an exemplar, 'This,' we would say, 'is how to write a novel that is impossible to forget.'"   —*Commercial Appeal*

"A heart-rending novel."   —*Boston Herald*

"A nightmare limned in gold."   —*Entertainment Weekly*

Praise for EVERYONE'S PRETTY

"With a sharp eye for small details, a keen sense of the absurd and strong empathy for its creations, *Everyone's Pretty* is both prism and truth."   —*Washington Post Book World*

"A kaleidoscopic new satire of America's quietly freakish office workers . . . gives voice to a wide variety of life's unbeautiful losers—and makes them sing for us."   —*Boston Globe*

"A biting send-up of vapid Americana wrapped up in a hilarious novel about five desperate Angelenos in search of redemption."   —*Boldtype*

"Juggling an enormous cast of psychos, *Everyone's Pretty* revels in its own religious chaos, the sexually crazed repeatedly clashing with the sexually pure . . . The book impressively teeters on the edge of total inanity, each scene becoming increasingly uncomfortable, then unraveling out of control."   —*Village Voice*

"*Everyone's Pretty* is so transgressive, so wildly and beautifully dark, that it's like a breath of fresh air in a stale literary environment over-run with too-clever postmodernists." —*Tucson Weekly*

| Also by Lydia Millet |

Omnivores

George Bush, Dark Prince of Love

My Happy Life

Everyone's Pretty

Oh Pure and Radiant Heart

How the Dead Dream

Love in Infant Monkeys

Lydia Millet

| *stories* |

Soft Skull Press
New York

Copyright © 2009 by Lydia Millet. All rights reserved under International and Pan-American Copyright Conventions.

This is a work of fiction. Names, characters, places, and incidents are the product of the author's imagination or are used fictitiously. Any resemblance to actual persons, living or dead, is entirely coincidental.

Library of Congress Cataloging-in-Publication Data is available.

ISBN: 978-1-59376-252-0

Cover design by Jamie Keenan
Interior design by Neuwirth & Associates, Inc.
Illustrations by Sharon McGill

Printed in the United States of America

Soft Skull Press
1140 Broadway, Suite 704
New York, NY 10001

www.softskull.com

Distributed by Publishers Group West

10 9 8 7 6

| Contents |

Love in Infant Monkeys

Sexing the Pheasant

WHEN A BIRD LANDED on her foot the pop star was surprised. She had shot it, certainly, with her gun. Then it fell from the sky. But she had not expected the actual death thing. Its beak spurted blood. She'd never really noticed birds. Though one reviewer had compared her to a screeching harpy. That was back when she was starting. What an innocent child she was then. She'd actually gone and looked it up at the library. "One of several loathsome, voracious monsters. They have the head of a woman and the wings and claws of a bird."

She did not appreciate the term *pop star*. She had told this to Larry King. She preferred *performance artist*. She was high art and low commodity, and ironic about how perfectly the two fit. A blind man could see her irony.

She was postmodern, if you wanted to know, pastiche. She embodied.

What, exactly?

If you had to ask, you just didn't get it.

The bird feebly flapped and made silent beak-openings. Where the hell was Guy when she needed him? The London tabloids still called him Mr. Madonna, even though she had tried to make clear on numerous occasions that he wore the testicles in the family. She wanted to yell at them: Giant testicles, OK? Testicles! Huge! ("Large bollocks." Use frequently.) He was back there somewhere in the trees. Easy to get separated on a thousand acres. She was an English lady now, not to the manor born, but to the manor ascended. So she was the American ideal, which was the self-made person, and the English ideal too, which was snotty aristocrats. Not bad for a girl from Pontiac, Michigan. These days she just said "the Midwest," which gave it more of a cornfed feeling. Wholesome. In that *Vogue* thing she said Guy was "laddish" and she was "cheeky" and Midwestern. Later she learned "laddish" was pretty much an insult, actually. Well, eff 'em if they couldn't take a joke.

She should step on its little head and crunch it. But the boots were Prada.

Should she shoot it again? No. She couldn't stand to. Sorry. She would just wait for the rest of them; no point being out here all alone anyway. Shouldn't have strutted off all righteous while they stood there drinking. If he wanted to be a frat boy, let him. Her own body was a hallowed temple. His was apparently more of a bordello/ sewer type thing. He was acting out because he was pissed at her. (Self: "peevish." *Pissed* meant drunk here.) For the shrunken-balls situation. No man wanted puny shriveled ones the size of Bing cherries. Still—not her fault. He had to step up himself. If he felt like the stay-at-home wife to her world-famous superstar, he had serious work to do. On himself. Not on her. She was not the one with the self-esteem issues.

Frankly she might as well be doing weights, if the alternative was standing around in the dried-out brown winter grass waiting for idiots. Waste of time. Hers was at a premium. And the abs were a perfect washboard, but in her personal opinion the quads could still use some hardening.

When the rest of the party got here he would take care of it for her. Drunk or sober, he would put it out of its misery. What were men good for if not to crush the last spark of life out of a small helpless creature?

OK. The rabbi had been hinting at this: It was better not to kill animals. For sport, anyway. Before, when she was learning to shoot, she never hit anything. Only the clay pigeons. It was fun and games then. The "bespoke" clothes were good, the whole "compleat" attitude. (Good thinking.) These knee breeches, for instance, were the sh–t. She bent over and stared at them. Flattering. She was "chuffed." (Self! So good!) And guns, let's face it: There was no better prop in the world. A woman with a gun was kind of a man in girls' clothes, a transvestite with an external dildo. But guns had more finesse. A gun was basically a huge iron dildo designed by someone French and classy.

So, shooting: She had liked it till now. Guy looked good with his 12-bore. He was a nature boy. It was sexy on him, esp. with the faux-Cockney stylings. ("Mockney." Use in moderation.) Basically if a man had a gun it was like a double cock. A cock and a replica cock, which was also postmodern. One had the power of life, the other had the power of death. Yin-yang. *Sefirot*. Etc.

Back to the bird. She felt a wince in her throat. It was still struggling weakly and blubbing blood, trying to flap its way up a small rise in the ground. Not much time had passed. All this thinking made the minutes go by slowly. Had she kicked it away? She must have just stepped back. It wasn't on the tip of her boot anymore; it was a few inches off, dry leaves sticking to its bloody side as it wobbled forward and then did a faceplant. Must have a leg broken, as well as a wing. Guess she had good aim these days, since she'd really hit it. Madonna, marksman. That worked. Evoked paintings from the Renaissance. ("Re-*nay*-since." Use frequently.) Gentle mother of God done in a Duccio style, or a soft Da Vinci: But then, instead of holding the Christ child, sweetly cradling an AK-47.

Consider for next album.

Madge, marksman. That worked too. When the British press gave you a nickname, that meant you were one of their own. Love you or hate you, that was irrelevant. What mattered was being one of them. In the gray steely ranks. The long-gone colonies. Once they ruled the world, now all they had was a better accent. They wore it well, though. An entire country that was basically quaint. Plus less of them were obese. In her closets there were hundreds of those tailor-made tweeds . . . but she could still wear the outfits, even if she stopped the killing. Right? You could pull off tweed without actually shooting. Couldn't you?

Esther, marksman . . . nah. Didn't work.

She was cold, standing there shivering. If millions of screaming fans knew she was cold at this very instant, they would rush to her aid. They would bring her their coats. Take the coats off their backs. Yeah, whatever. One thing was for sure: Their coats would suck. (Off-the-rack = "naff." Use frequently.)

It had to be dying soon. "Shite!" (Good work, self!) It was taking a while.

She had nothing against the poor thing, but then it rose out of the bushes and flew up and *blam*!—fell to Earth, like Bowie in that seventies movie. (Sternly to self: "Film.") He was like Jesus in that. If Jesus was an alien. Which, let's face it, he probably was. There was no other explanation. Huh: What if Christians were basically the UFOlogists of ancient history? And the Jews were the people who were the debunkers? They were like, "No, the Messiah hasn't come, and if he has, where's the proof?" Whereas the Christians were the ones who said, "Seriously, the aliens came down, and we saw them. Man, you've got to believe us!" Except there was only one of these aliens, namely Jesus.

Christians were hopeful, which made them basically insane. They were hopeful about the past. I.e.,

Christ = son of God, etc. Hopeful about the future. I.e., paradise will be ours, etc. And then the clincher: They figured this particular hope made them legitimate. They hoped they personally would be saved and live happily ever after—and then they had the chutzpah to call that faith. So like, faith was thinking you were great and deserved to sit at the right hand of God. Selfish much?

Jews were more like, Come on. Be reasonable. Here we are on Earth, now just try to be nice for five minutes, would you? Can we have five lousy minutes without a genocide? Sheesh.

Course Kabbalah was something else again. It wasn't that you deserved to be saved, it was that God was in *you*. The power of the names of God, the seventy-two names inscribed in figures of light . . . what if the bird had tiny eggs in a nest somewhere? She had her own eggs, Lola and Rocco. This thing could be a mother too. Poor little thing. Birds were graceful. She wouldn't look that good if someone shot her. Bad thought! Knock on wood. She reached out for a thin tree. Did a tree count as wood? I mean yeah, she knew that, but for luck purposes?

Actually, if she was shot in the right place, then well

lit, she could look excellent. Kind of a martyr concept. Consider. If not shot, crucified. Good one there.

Now the eggs would die in the abandoned nest, forgotten. But maybe not, if this bird was a man. Rooster, that is. When it came to pheasants, they called them hens and roosters. (Good work, self.) Too bad she couldn't tell. You couldn't check between a bird's legs like with a dog or a horse, nosirree. A male bird had nothing out there bobbing and dangling. Really no way to know. Unless you were, like, a bird-penis specialist. (Kidding, self.) The poor birds had no dicks. Their sex was in the plumage. Any idiot knew that. Different colors, she guessed, but then there were the young ones that all looked the same. Piece in the *Mirror* had recently called her "an accomplished breeder of pheasant and partridge"—good. Good. In the sense of *manager*, she *managed* the breeding. She didn't sex the things personally—so what? She hired very good gamekeepers. Delegation was key.

She was chosen by God. That was what so many people seemed to completely overlook. What else explained her meteoric rise to stardom? Her continued success? For twenty years now she had basically been a megastar. Try the most famous person in the world, basically.

They said her name in the same breath with *Elvis* and *Marilyn*. What, because she was pretty? Just because she could dance and had mastered a Casio? (Kidding, self, just kidding!) She had talent, even brilliance, even exceptional brilliance ("brill"—use in moderation), and nothing's wrong with a Casio anyway. The eighties were the eighties.

But that alone would get you to the corner gas station. ("Petrol." Good thinking.) True to her name, which was not even a fake one, she had been chosen. Chosen to embody.

Now and then someone, usually a crazed psycho, asked: "Are you the Second Coming?" Because that was what it looked like, if you were literal-minded. Like maybe she was the Mother of God, Mark II. She wouldn't go that far, of course. There was a reason they called them psychos. But the kind of luck she'd had couldn't really be called luck anymore. Luck was catching a bus, maybe winning a raffle. Luck was a good parking spot.

You had to keep this kind of knowledge under wraps, though, as a celebrity. You had to keep it a secret between yourself and yourself or you would end up a Tom Cruise. Believing the sun shone out of your sphincter, beaming with the smugness of an All-Knowing Colon.

When all you were, at the end of the day, was a highly paid face.

But she got him, basically, the whole Scientology thing. Not her "cup of tea" (good work, self!) but what the media didn't get, when they made fun of her and Guy for Kabbalah, or Gere for his Dalai Lama or Cruise for his pyramid scheme or whatever the *Dianetics* thing was, was that *you* needed to worship too. The fans worshipped you because they needed something—well, what were *you* supposed to do? Well, prostrate yourself before the Infinite. Clearly.

OK, granted, sometimes the mirror suggested it: Not your fault if your reflection reminded you of all that was sacred, all that was divine and holy. The world would do it to you. At that point you were the victim. Brainwashing, like with anorexics. Too many magazine covers. But she resisted. She was actually very humble. And of course, it was not wrong to see God in yourself. Anyone could do it. That was where the intellectual part came in. She read the holy books, she read old plays and that . . . it helped her, as an artist, to be extremely intelligent. Besides being a savvy businesswoman—she got that a lot, and rightly—and even a genius at the marketing level, she was a seeker. A seeker never gives up.

She was pretty sure she remembered there was some kind of bird that would sit on another bird's eggs, hatch them and feed them like they were its own. The Mia Farrow of nature. Maybe one of those little mama-birds would come rescue the eggs of the dying one. She hoped so. Other day she'd seen that pigeon she told *Vogue* was the reincarnation of Cecil Beaton . . . The best fags were all English fags. Englishmen were the Ur-faggots, pretty much. All other fags in the world were pale imitations of real English fags. This was the land of homos; even the straight men were fags here. One reason she liked it so much. In the U.S. guys were basically rapists; here they seemed uptight and formal, with their great accents and not show-ing any emotion, but all the time they were basically daydreaming about nancy boys in sailor suits. Not all of them, of course—I mean, what would a sex goddess like her do without at least a few of the poor "sods" (pat to self!) being genuine heteros but, you know, the default position. ("Benders, bum bandits, ginger beer." Use in moderation.)

Guy was not gay, of course. But he had an edge of

anger to him. The ones that weren't gay were often angry about it.

It was a trade-off, more or less.

OK. The bird was finally chilling out. Lying there. Effin' dead.

"Oi. Bag one, then?"

She jumped. He'd snuck up right behind her. It was the red-faced "bloke" from "down the pub," Guy's new pet "lager lout." (*Self! Ex*cellent!) Pig, as far as she knew. Gave her the creeps. What Guy saw in these losers from the King John with their saggy beer tits . . . Come to think of it, she liked this one even less when he was carrying a gun. A gun was like a cigarette that way: If you already looked good, it made you look better; if you looked crap to begin with, it made you look even worse. This particular "lager boy" had a chip on his shoulder about women with power. It hung on him like a stink. Made him actually dangerous.

Best not to challenge him. Alone here in the middle of the woods.

"I guess, you know—actually, I feel pretty bad. You know? I mean, it was really suffering."

"Brain the size of a peanut, yeah? How much suffering could there be?"

He was openly contemptuous. Thing about these lager boys of Guy's was, they gave her a reality check. Like, what would it be like to be a regular person again? They had zero respect for her, for her megastar stature. At this point in her career, most people she met either had to resist an urge to genuflect or got completely tongue-tied. Often their mouths hung open like Down syndrome kids'. (Which was sad. The real retards, that is. Come to think of it, retards were among the few who still acted normal.) Once she had cheek-kissed a journalist—one, two, in the English manner—and he'd fainted and soiled himself all over the place. And that was a guy who was used to famous people; they were his total job. You learned to spot in a second which ones were going to freak out. Point was, the lager louts would have been refreshing if they weren't such assholes. She was sorry for their wives and girlfriends.

He leaned down to pick it up.

"No! No," she said, and put out her hand. "Just—thanks, but you can leave it. I want to just leave it there."

"Defeats the purpose, dunnit."

"I just want to leave it in peace. I don't want to desecrate the corpse."

He snorted.

"You seen the others? Guy? Was he with you?"

"Nah. Went off on me own." He was turning away.

"Wait! Can you tell me something?"

"Mmm?"

"Is it a hen? Or—"

"Rooster! Blimey."

What a relief. No eggs.

He stumped back down the hill, head shaking. Good riddance. She knelt down beside the small body, modest hump of brown and red feathers. It was still beautiful. She put her hand on the feathers. You could feel the slight warm frame beneath them. It was light, almost nothing in there. Birds were like air.

It had been more beautiful when it wasn't dead, though. Before it was shot. Which wasn't true of everyone. Take JFK, even John Lennon. Assassination had matured them like a fine pinot. If you died of old age, besides not leaving a good-looking corpse, all you died for in the end was living. But if you got shot, you were an instant symbol. You must have died *for* something.

She was always completely new; that was her secret, albeit an open one. Sure, it was obvious, but no one did it like she did. None of them could touch her when it came to transformation. That was the secret to her longevity. She wasn't one megastar; she was a new one constantly. Novelty was what people lived for. Skin-deep, maybe, but so what? Skin was the biggest organ.

She should envy the bird, actually. Guy said in the wild they died of starvation. Shooting them was a mercy killing. I mean come on—fly, eat worms, fly, lay eggs, fly, starve to death. "Bob's your uncle." (You go girl.) Life was not equal for everyone. That was another reason she liked it better in England. They didn't stand for that Thomas Paine bullshit here, all men were created equal, etc. What a crock. One drive through Alabama was all you needed to take the bloom off that rose. One ride on the subway. (Self: "Tube." Easy.) Back home, the second you stepped out of a major city you were surrounded by the remnants of Early Man. Here there were some of those, too, but you had to go down the pub to find them. And at least they didn't run the country.

All history was the history of class struggle, right? Lenin said that, and he had style. He had a very sharp look. Good tailoring. When the statues came down, she for one was sorry. She always wanted to meet him.

Maybe if she said a prayer. Yes. It felt right.

She touched the red string and squatted beside the

bird. She would think holy thoughts about it; she would utter a name of God. She closed her eyes with her fingers resting on the feathers.

This was a problem she had: When she wasn't already tired, it was sometimes hard to speed-meditate. Mind kept working, working. A powerful machine. Difficult to rein in. The bird once ate the worms, now worms would eat the bird . . . every word filled with light. That was how it should be. Desire to Receive. Which name? The name to reduce negativity?

What would help her and Guy, she saw, besides going to the Centre together on a more regular basis, was if Guy understood her more on a spiritual level. If he could just see her interior the way she saw it herself, he would not worry about the shrinking mini-Bings. He would see she was a little girl, secretly. She was a Shirley Temple. She was very pure, despite her sophistication. She believed in the ten luminous emanations. The ladder of awareness. She cherished in the core of herself the beingness of being.

Immortality for the bird, for all things of beauty. That was what the lager louts could just never *capiche*. It was right, so right, to know your own beauty and see it was God's own beauty too. One day the body would be a giving vessel, not just a receiving. Life could go on forever. They might not be able to understand, the lager louts, what she was, what all of them could be if they gave themselves over to the light instead of, say, the Guinness, but that did not mean there was not room in God for them too. The house of God had many rooms. And through the great windows of these rooms, the golden beams of the divine streamed in.

Not as many rooms as Ashcombe, possibly. Joke! Joke to self. The house of God was never-ending.

The word for healing . . . ?

But you couldn't heal dead.

She rose, still looking down at the bird. It was peaceful at last. She had killed it, but she was also sorry. In the end, that was all that mattered. Do not have violence in your heart.

"I love you now," she said.

She heard voices and turned. The hunting party stood at the edge of the trees, too far away to distinguish. But she thought she saw Guy with them. Nearby stood the dogs, their tails wagging. The men's faces were small white blurs. She saw hands raise. First she thought they were raised in greeting, hailing her from afar. She raised her own right arm and waved back. But then she caught flashes of silver in the sun. Flasks raised to their faces. One of them stepped back from the group, staggering and falling. They had apparently not ceased to drink the whole time. Their laughter was carrying.

She felt annoyed, but then a surge of forgiving. She could not blame them for their alcoholism. They were so small! All of them. Pity warmed her, a generous blossoming. It was so hard to be small.

Girl and Giraffe

THE MAN CALLED GEORGE Adamson lived a long life, long and rough and most of it in the African bush. He set up house in a tent with a thatch roof and dirt floor, full of liquor and books. He smoked a pipe with a long stem, sported a white goatee and went around bare-chested in khaki shorts—a small, fit man, deeply tanned. He was murdered in his eighty-third year by Somali lion poachers.

Joy Adamson, his wife and the author of *Born Free*, had been stabbed to death a few years before. She bled out alone, on the road where she fell. They were somewhat estranged by the time of Joy's death. They had cats instead of children—George had raised scores of lions, while Joy had moved on from lions to cheetahs to leopards—and lions and leopards could not cohabit, so George and Joy lived apart. They maintained contact, but they were hundreds of miles distant.

Two of George's adoptive children, Girl and Boy, had come to live with him in the early nineteen-sixties. This was in Kenya, where the Second Battalion of the Scots Guards was stationed to fight a mutiny in Dar-es-Salaam. It was the tail end of the British empire in East Africa.

When Girl and Boy were nine months old, the Scots Guards brought them to the plains beneath Mount Kenya, to a farm where a British company was filming *Born Free*. Along with twenty-two other lions, Girl and Boy had roles in the movie. Afterward most of the lions were sent to zoos, where they would live out their lives in narrow spaces. But Girl and Boy were given to Adamson, who had become attached to them during filming. He took them to a place named Meru, where he made a camp.

Meru was in red-earth country, with reticulated giraffes browsing among the acacia and thornbush. Zebras roamed in families and the odd solitary rhino passed through the brush; there were ostriches, too, and an aging elephant named Rudkin, who plundered tomatoes.

Girl was one of Adamson's success stories whereas her brother, Boy, was an extravagant failure; yet Boy was the one that Adamson deeply loved.

Girl had been fed all her life, but she took readily to the hunt. Her first kill was a jeering baboon, her second an eland with a broken leg, her third a baby zebra. From there she took down a full-grown cow eland and was soon accomplished. Meanwhile Boy did not feel moved to kill for himself; he merely feasted off the animals she brought down.

So Girl became a wild lion, but Boy did not. Boy remained close to Adamson all his life, often in camp, between two worlds. Though he made forays into the wild, he did not vanish within it. And on one occasion, hanging around camp while people were visiting, he stuck his head into a jeep and bit the arm of a seven-year-old boy. This boy was the son of the local park warden; soon an order came down for Boy's execution.

But before Adamson could carry out the shooting—he was busy protesting to bureaucrats, who declined to listen—Boy was found under a bush with a porcupine quill through one eye and a broken leg. If not euthanized on the spot he would have to be moved; so Adamson sat on the ground beside him until the veterinarian could fly in, by turns drinking whiskey, brandishing his rifle and sleeping.

After triage in camp Adamson prepared for an airlift to a better-equipped facility. He and Boy would live on a private estate of Joy's while he nursed the animal back to health. And as they were loading the lion into Adamson's pickup for the airstrip, Girl—though she had barely seen her brother for a year—emerged suddenly from the bush. She jumped onto the back of the truck, where Boy lay sedated and wrapped in a blanket. No one was able to entice her away, so they began the drive to the airstrip with Girl along for the ride.

But on the way she spotted a young giraffe by the road and became distracted. She jumped off the pickup. She was a wild lion now, and wild lions are hungry.

That was the last time Adamson saw Girl and the last time she saw any of them. Later, when Adamson returned to Meru, he would search for her fruitlessly.

Boy grew irritable in temperament after the surgery, due to the steel rod in his leg: And who among us might not become cantankerous? Two years after he and Girl were parted, he suddenly attacked a man named Stanley who had tended him with gentle care through illness and injury. Adamson heard a scream and went running with his rifle to find that Boy had bitten deep into Stanley's shoulder; he turned and shot his beloved lion through the heart and then tended to his friend, who bled to death from a severed jugular inside ten minutes.

In Adamson's autobiography the end of Boy is well described, while the end of Girl, who lived out her days in the wild, is invisible. Happy endings often are.

But there is one more report of Girl outside Adamson's published writings. It was made by a man who claimed to have visited Adamson in his camp the year before his murder, one Stefan Juncker based in Tübingen, Germany. Juncker said he had made a pilgrimage to see Adamson at Kora, where he was living with his final lions. Since Adamson constantly welcomed guests to his camp, such a visit would not have been uncommon.

The two men sat beside a fire one night and Adamson— in his cups, which the German implied was not rare— became melancholy. He remembered a time when he had not been alone, before his wife and his brother had died. He remembered his old companions, sitting there at the base of the hills among the boulders and the thornbush; he remembered all his lions, his women and his men.

His brother Terence, who had lived with him at Kora, had in his dotage discovered that he had what Adamson called "a talent for divining." By wielding a swinging pendulum over a map, he could determine the location of lost or wanted things. This included water, missing persons and lions, which he correctly located about 60 percent of the time. Adamson was skeptical in theory, not being much given to magical thinking, but had to admit that his brother's method led him to his lions faster than spoor- or radio-based tracking. It was inexplicable, he said, but there it was.

Since Terence had died of an embolism two years before, Adamson no longer had a diviner.

At this point Adamson gestured toward a flower bush a few feet away. That was where Terence lay now, he said. And there, he said, turning, over there by a tree was dear Boy's grave; he had buried his favorite lion himself, though others had dug up the corpse later to see proof that he was dead. He had been forced to rebury him several times.

The German was disturbed. He did not like the fact that Adamson had laid his brother to rest a stone's throw from a killer.

There was much that science had not yet understood,

went on Adamson, about the minds of lions and men and how they might meet. Divining was one example—had the lions somehow told Terence where they could be found?—but he had also known others. In fact, he said, he would tell of an odd event he had once witnessed. Over the years he had thought of it now and then, he said; and at this point a warm, low wind sprang up from the Tana River and blew out the embers of their campfire, sinking them into darkness.

He had thought of it over the years, he repeated, but he had mentioned it to no one. He would tell it, if the German could keep a secret.

Of course, lied the German.

It was when he was first taking Girl out to hunt. This was in Meru, he said, in the mid-nineteen-sixties. Of course now, more than twenty years later, Girl would have to be long dead.

All your stories end with someone dead, said the German.

All *my* stories? asked Adamson.

He and Girl had been walking through the forest together and had emerged into a clearing, where they surprised a herd of giraffes browsing. The herd quickly took off, galloping away before Adamson had a chance to count them, but they left behind a gangly foal without the sense to run. Perfect prey. It should fall easily. It stood stupidly, blinking, backed up against a large tree.

Girl charged, with Adamson standing by proudly. She had made several kills in the preceding days and he considered her a prodigy.

But abruptly she stopped, pulling up short. Her ears were flat; then they pricked. She and the foal seemed to be studying each other. Adamson was shocked, bordering on indignant, but he remained in the copse. Possibly Girl sensed something wrong with the giraffe, he thought; or possibly there were other predators behind it, competition in the form of a clan of hyenas he could not see.

As he waited Girl stood unmoving, crouched a few feet from her quarry. Then the giraffe reached up slowly and mouthed a branch with its mobile, rubbery lips. It chewed.

Adamson was flabbergasted. Possibly the animal recognized his lion as a neophyte hunter: But how could it? Giraffes were not insightful; they had the dullness of most placid grazers. Either way, the animal should be bolting. Girl would be on him in a second, fast as light.

He could see Girl only from the rear; her tail twitched,

her shoulders hunched. He could not see her face, which frustrated him, he told the German, for a lion's face is extraordinary in its capacity for expression. What was she waiting for?

Then again, he thought, as he watched the stillness between them and held his own breath, the foal was going nowhere. Maybe Girl was hypnotized by the future: Maybe she saw the arc of her own leap, was already feeling the exhilaration of flight and the impact, the smell and weight of the foal as it crumpled beneath her, as she dragged and wrestled and tore it down, worried the tough hide and sweet flesh. Possibly she was waiting, pent up and ready.

But no. Girl straightened; she relaxed. She sniffed around the foal's long legs. She jumped onto a dry log. She yawned.

And the giraffe kept eating, munching and grunting softly. It shifted on its feet; it stooped down, head dipping toward Girl and up again to the branches, where it tore and chewed, tore and chewed, with a complacent singularity of purpose.

There was sun on the log, glancing across the nape of the lion's neck so that her face was illuminated, the rest of her in shadow. She licked a paw and lay down.

Adamson, squatting in the bushes, stayed put. His body was still but his mind worked hard, puzzling. He considered giraffes. Terence had a weakness for elephants; himself, he was strictly a lion man. But giraffes, though morphological freaks, had never interested either of them. Artiodactyla, for one thing: the order of camel, swine and bovids. Not suited for long-term relationships. Strictly for riding, eating or milking, really. He pitied them, but not much. There were no refrigerators in nature, after all; meat and milk had to keep themselves fresh.

After years in the bush he saw all animals as predators or prey. The tourists that came through his camp wanting to pet the lions? Now those were strictly prey, he mused.

Then, recalled to the present after a pause: No offense.

None taken, said the German heartily.

In fact the German had felt a prickle of annoyance. The flight in, on a single-engine Cessna in jolting turbulence, had made him squeeze his eyes shut and pray silently to a God in whom he did not believe. For this?

An old alcoholic, he thought angrily, with poor hygiene—that was all. He had been eight years of age when he saw *Born Free*, living in a claustrophobic bourgeois household in Stuttgart. His father was fat as blood sausage and his mother used a bottle of hairspray a week. He thought Adamson and his beautiful wife were like Tarzan and Jane.

But Kirsten had disapproved of this trip, and she was probably right: nothing more than a midlife crisis.

The smoke from Adamson's pipe was spicy. The German was disgusted by smoking—frankly, any man fool enough to do it deserved what he got—but he had to admit the pipe smelled far better than cigarettes.

You were saying, the German reminded him. Girl and giraffe?

Yes, said Adamson softly.

The old man was frail, thought the German, with the ranginess of a hungry dog; his muscles had no flesh between them. He had nothing to spare.

So Girl had lain there on the log in the sun, dozing while the giraffe moved from tree to tree. The sun crossed the sky and clouds massed, casting a leaden grayness over the low hills. Adamson stayed seated in the scrub, drank from a flask and puffed on his pipe. There was a silver elegance to the day, which was unusually mild and breezy; he listened to the wind rattle the branches and whisper the dry grass. Birds alit in the trees and moved off—he noticed mostly black-headed weavers and mourning doves—and Girl and the giraffe ignored them. The shadows grew longer; the sun was sinking. Adamson began to feel impatient, pulled back to camp. He had things he should do before dark.

It was almost dusk when the giraffe moved. It ambled over and bent its head to Girl again, who stirred.

While it is not true, said Adamson solemnly to the German, that giraffes never lie down, as legend has it, it *is* true that they do so rarely and for a very short time. And never, he said, in his experience, did they lie down at the feet of their predators.

And yet this was what the foal did.

It had been a good day, said Adamson, and raised his glass.

As he talked, the German had built up the fire again, and now he saw the flames reflecting off amber. He was regretting his choice. The choice had been between Africa or Mallorca, where his wife was now suntanning.

The foal lay down deliberately, said Adamson, right beside the dry log. It was deliberate.

And Girl stretched her legs, as a cat will do, luxurious and long, all four straight out at their fullest reach like table legs. She stretched and rose, jumped languidly off the log and paused. Then she leaned down over the foal and sank in her teeth.

The movement, said Adamson, was gentle. The foal barely struggled; its legs jerked reflexively but soon it was still.

Later, he said, he almost believed he had dreamed the episode. But he came to believe, over the years, that a call and answer had passed between Girl and the giraffe: the foal had asked for and been granted reprieve. Girl had given him a whole afternoon in which to feel the thorny branches and leaves in his mouth, the sun and shade cross his neck, his heavy lashes blink in the air.

It was a free afternoon, because all afternoon the foal had been free of the past and free of the future. Completely free.

It was almost, said Adamson, as though the possibilities of the world had streamed through Girl and the giraffe: And he, a hunched-over primate in the bushes, had been the dumb one, with his insistent frustration at that which he could not easily fathom, his restless, churning efforts to achieve knowledge. Being a primate, he watched; being a primate, he was separate forever. The two of them opened up beyond all he knew of their natures, suspended. They were fluid in time and space, and between them flowed the utter acceptance of both of their deaths.

They had been together, said Adamson, closer than he had ever been to anyone. They had given; they had given; they had shimmered with spirit.

Spirits, thought the German, glancing at the luminous dial of his watch: yes indeed. Bushmill's, J&B, Ballantine, Cutty Sark and Glenlivet on special occasions.

This was in Kenya in the late nineteen-eighties, decades after the Mau Mau rebellion brought the deaths of two hundred whites and twenty thousand blacks. A new homespun corruption had replaced the old foreign repression; fewer and fewer lions roamed the grasslands of East Africa, and the British were long gone.

Sir Henry

THE DOG WAS SERIOUS, always had been. No room for levity. Those around him might be lighthearted. Often they laughed, sometimes even at his expense—the miniature size, bouncing gait, flopping ears. He was a dachshund. Not his fault. You were what you were. He would have preferred the aspect of an Alsatian, possibly a Norwegian elkhound. He viewed himself as one of these large and elegant breeds.

This much could be seen with the naked eye, and the dogwalker saw it. The dogwalker was also serious—a loner, except for dogs. He prided himself on his work. He had no patience for moonlighters, for the giddy girls talking on their cell phones as they tottered through Sheep Meadow with seven different-size purebreds on as many leashes, jerking them this way and that and then screeching in indignation when the dogs became confused. He had once seen such a girl get two fingers ripped off. He'd called 911 himself. It was an ugly scene. The paramedics recovered the fingers, snarled up in leather and nylon, but the hand had been twisted so roughly they predicted it would never work right. The girl herself had passed out long before the ambulance got there. Turned out she was premed at Columbia.

Two of the dogs were also injured. Their mutual aggression had caused the accident in the first place; he had seen it coming all the way from the carousel—the dogs straining and nipping at each other, the girl on her phone with the leashes tangled around her left hand.

Himself, he was a professional with exacting standards. He made an excellent living. He had subcontractors, yes, but all of them were vet techs, trainers or groomers at the very least. None were college girls who took the job literally, expecting it to be a simple walk in the park.

The dogwalker gave his charges respect as he saw fit. Some did not deserve it, and they did not receive it. To these frivolous or problem dogs he gave only the curt nod of discipline. His favorite dogs had a sense of dignity. Theirs was a mutual approbation. Sir Henry was one of these.

The owner traveled constantly, often in Europe, Asia or South America. All over. He was a performer of some kind, in show business. When he was in town he spent most of his time at the gym, maintaining his physique, tanning, shopping or seeking photo opportunities. The dogwalker barely registered him. The dogwalker went to get Sir Henry three times a day, rain or shine. Henry seldom went out otherwise—the odd trip with one of the girls when they were home from school, or the wife on the rare occasion when she was not, like the entertainer, at the gym or shopping. Now and then, if he found himself at loose ends for twenty minutes or so, the entertainer paraded with Sir Henry personally, scoping the park for other celebs to do the meet and greet with. In the puppy days he had taken Sir Henry out frequently, but the puppy days had passed.

There was an older dachshund, Precious, also owned by the entertainer, but Precious had been virtually adopted by one of the domestics, an illegal from Haiti if the dogwalker was not mistaken. The Haitian took Precious out on her cigarette breaks. But not Sir Henry.

The dogwalker walked Sir Henry alone or with

one particular other dog, a small poodle belonging to a dying violinist. The poodle was stately, subtle and, like the dachshund, possessed of a poise that elevated it beyond its miniature stature. The two seemed to have an understanding. The poodle marked first and with great discretion; the dachshund marked second. They trotted happily beside each other at an identical pace, despite the fact that the poodle's legs were almost twice as long. They listened to the dogwalker acutely and responded promptly to his commands. It was their pleasure to serve.

Did they serve him? No, and he would not have it so. They served decorum, the order of things.

At times the dogwalker enjoyed resting with them; he would settle down on a park bench and the dogs would sit at his feet, paws together neatly, looking forward with an appearance of vigilance. Their heads turned in unison as other dogs passed.

When it was morning, noon and night, of course, as it was with Sir Henry, it was no longer merely walking. The dogwalker was in loco parentis. It was he who had discovered the bladder infection, the flea eggs. It was he who had recommended a vet, a diet, routine. In the economy of dogwalkers he was top tier; only the exceptionally wealthy could afford him, those who did not even notice that their dogwalking fees exceeded rents in Brooklyn. His personal service included a commitment of the heart, for which the megarich were willing to pay through the nose. About his special charges he was not workmanlike in the least. He was professional, operating by a mature code with set rules for all of his employees, but he was not slick. He did not cultivate in himself the distancing practiced by pediatric oncologists and emergency-room surgeons. His clients sensed this, and where their pets were concerned, his fond touch soothed the conscience.

He began with respect and often ended with love. When a dog was taken from him—a move, a change of fortune or, in one painful case, a spontaneous gift-ing—he felt it deeply. His concern for a lost dog, as he thought of them, would keep him up for many nights after one of these incidents. When a young Weimaraner was lost to him with not even a chance to say good-bye, he remained deeply angry for weeks. The owner, a teenage heiress often featured in the local tabloids, had given his charge away on the spur of the moment to a Senegalese dancer she met at a restaurant. He had no doubt that drug use was involved. The dog, a timid, damaged animal of great gentleness and forbearance, was on a plane to Africa by the time he found out about it the next day.

The loss was hard for him. He was tormented by thoughts of the sweet-natured bitch cowering, subjected to the whims of an unkind owner or succumbing to malnutrition. Of course, there was a chance the new owner was thoughtful, attentive, nurturing—but he had no reason to expect such a happy outcome. In his work he saw shockingly few people who were fit for their dogs.

Walking Sir Henry and the poodle up Cherry Hill, he remembered the Weimaraner, and a pang of grief and regret glanced through him. It had been almost three years ago; where was the good creature now? He had looked up Senegal on the Internet after she was taken. "Senegal is a mainly low-lying country, with a semidesert area to the north . . ." He had never been to Africa, and in his mind the Weimaraner lived alternately in the squalor of dusty famine, scrabbling for scraps of food among fly-eyed hungry children, or in the cool white majesty of minarets. There were obdurate camels and palm trees near the Weimaraner, or there were UN cargo planes dropping crates of rice.

In less colorful moments, he was quietly certain the

Weimaraner was dead. The incident had taught him a valuable lesson, one he firmly believed he should have learned earlier: In the client-selection process, people must be subjected to far greater scrutiny than their dogs. He no longer contracted with unreliable owners. If he had reason to suspect an owner or family was not prepared to keep a dog for its lifetime, he did not take the job.

It could be difficult. Sometimes a dog owned by one of these irresponsible persons had powerful appeal—grace, sensitivity, an air of loneliness. But the risk was too great. He made himself walk away from these dogs.

Sir Henry emitted one short bark and he and the poodle stopped and stood, tails wagging, pointing to the left. The dogwalker stopped too. There was the violinist, wrapped in blankets, seated under a tree in his wheelchair with his attendant and an oxygen tank. The dogwalker was surprised. As far as he knew, the violinist, who was at the end stage of a long cancer, never came out of his penthouse anymore. The place had a large wraparound terrace from which the East River could be seen; there were potted trees and even a small lawn on this terrace, where the poodle spent much of its time.

"Blackie," said the violinist in his weak, rasping voice, and the dogwalker obediently let the two dogs approach.

"A surprise," said the dogwalker. He was not skilled at small talk.

"Figured I should take one last stroll in the park," said the violinist, and smiled. "Come here, Blackie."

The dogwalker handed the poodle's leash to the attendant and Blackie jumped up into his owner's lap. The old man winced but petted the poodle with a bone-stiff hand.

"I need to know what will happen to her," said the violinist. "When I die."

The dogwalker felt embarrassed. Death was an intimate subject. Yet it was close, and the violinist was quite right to plan for his dog.

"Difficult," he offered.

"I wonder if, if I were to establish a trust . . . ample provisions, financially . . . would you consider—?"

The dogwalker, surprised again, looked to the attendant who was holding the leash. She had a beseeching look on her face, and for a minute he did not know how to take this. Finally he decided the look meant the violinist would not be able to bear a flat-out refusal.

"Let me think," he said, stalling.

It was not in his code.

"Think fast," said the violinist, though he was still smiling.

"I will think about it overnight," said the dogwalker.

"You like Blackie," said the violinist, a quaver in his voice. "Right? Don't you like her?"

The dogwalker felt a terrible pity enfold him.

"Of course I do," he said quickly. "She is among my favorites."

The violinist, on the brink of tears, bent his head to his dog, petting her softly and rapidly as she patiently withstood the onslaught. His attendant shaded her own eyes and blinked into the distance.

"I am very attached to Blackie," the dogwalker bumbled on. "But the adoption of dogs is against my policy. Please give me till tomorrow."

"OK," said the violinist, and attempted to smile again. "I'll try not to kick the bucket before then."

"I would take her," explained the attendant, apologetic. "But I just can't."

She handed back the leash and Blackie jumped off the lap.

"We'll see you back at the apartment," called the attendant after him.

They had more than half an hour left on the circuit. As the dogs trotted in front of him, he saw Sir Henry turn back to the violinist, checking up on him.

If he accepted the dog, in a clear violation of established protocol, would his principles erode? Would he end up an eccentric with an apartment full of abandoned pets? By preferring dogs to humans he put himself at risk—myopia on the part of his fellow citizens of course, since dogs were so clearly their moral superiors. Still, he did not wish to be stigmatized.

As they neared the 72nd Street entrance he saw children approaching, delighted. Children were a matter of policy also. He allowed only quiet ones to touch his charges, and he preferred the females. Males made sudden movements, capered foolishly and often taunted.

He stopped now, for these were two melancholy slips of girls with round eyes.

"May I pet him, please?" asked one of them, and suspended a hand in the air over Sir Henry's head.

Sir Henry welcomed it. Girls reminded him of the entertainer's daughters, the dogwalker thought, two blond girls who had caressed him constantly when he was only three months old but now seemed unaware of his existence.

Himself, he was preoccupied; this was a critical decision. His mind wandered as the girls leaned down.
He gazed in their direction but he did not see them
clearly—bent pink forms with sunlight on wavy hair . . .
if he owned the poodle himself he could walk the dogs
like this every day, the dachshund and Blackie. Sir
Henry was most contented in the poodle's presence.

"You get *away*," said a woman harshly to the girls.
She wore tight leather pants and held a phone to her
ear. "They could bite. They're dirty."

"They are cleaner than you are," said the dogwalker
softly. "And they never bite nice little girls. Only mean
old witches."

"Right *now*," snapped the woman.

"Thanks, mister," said the elder girl, and looked with
longing at Sir Henry as the woman tugged at her arm.

He was often grateful that dogs had little use for language; still, they understood tone. The leather-pants
woman had slightly offended them, he suspected—a
telltale lowering of their heads as they made for the
gate. Dogs had an ear for the meaning in voice.

"Oh my God," said a fat man in front of them on the
path, pointing, and laughed. "It's David Hasselhoff."

He turned to see the entertainer advancing, talking

into his telephone and wearing what appeared to be gaudy jogging attire, a jacket with purple details that matched purple pants. No doubt he was on his way home from the gym.

Never before had the dogwalker run into two owners on a single walk.

"Yeah. Yeah," said David Hasselhoff on the phone. "Yeah. Yeah. Yeah." As he passed them he winked at the dogwalker, then swooped down, not stopping, to chuck Sir Henry on the chin. "Hey there, little buddy."

The dogwalker watched his back receding, ogled by various passersby. With his free hand the entertainer saluted them jauntily.

"The *Hoff*," said one, smirking.

"They love him in Germany," said another.

The dogwalker recalled hearing people on the sidewalk discuss the violinist also. "He did a recording for Deutsche Grammophon, the Tchaikovsky *Concerto in D*, that actually broke my heart." It was rare that he considered the lives of owners beyond their animals. To him they were dog neglecters most of all. And yet where would he be without this neglect?

The violinist, of course, could not be blamed in the least. He had insisted on walking Blackie himself when he was submitting to a barrage of chemotherapy that would have felled lesser men. The dogwalker respected the violinist, though it was unpleasant to see him in his wretchedness. A dog in his state would have been euthanized long ago.

In fact that was how he had met the violinist; the violinist had not gone through the usual channels. The dogwalker had come upon him struggling to keep up with Blackie on a path near Turtle Pond. Two kids on skateboards had almost run them over, and the old man had begun to tremble violently. His bones were like porcelain. Worse, one of the kids had called Blackie a "faggot dog" as he swooped away on his board. (At that time the poodle had sported an unfortunate Continental Clip with Hip Rosettes. Later, the dogwalker had persuaded the violinist to switch to a basic Lamb.)

But the skateboarder had infuriated him. Not the words, but what was behind them—malice directed at the dog. A senseless meanness of spirit. The poodle had never done anything to hurt the kid.

He had guided the frail old man to a ledge where he could sit, and from then on the poodle had been one of his charges.

He imagined telling the violinist he could not take

Blackie. In his mind he went over the conversation as he stood with the dogs. They were waiting for a walk signal.

"I am sorry," he would say. "But if I took in all the dogs, even all the dogs I like best, I would be a pet shelter, not a dogwalker."

The violinist would gaze at him sadly with his watery blue eyes. In his youth, the attendant had said once, the violinist had been quite handsome, and she'd shown him a black-and-white photograph. The violinist had survived a death camp, Stalin. Now his skin was like paper, his teeth yellow.

"Can't you make an exception?" the violinist might ask.

"I would like nothing more than to take Blackie in," he could say. "But all I can do is help find a new family for him. Allow me to do that, at least."

What bothered him was that the violinist had been so good to his dog. Such goodness should be rewarded.

If he did not take the poodle, chances were he would never see him again, once the violinist was out of the picture. The poodle would live out the rest of his days with someone who did not care for him as the violinist had. Blackie would be brokenhearted and Sir Henry would be bereft.

Of course even he, the dogwalker, could not promise to bestow upon the poodle the violinist's brand of solitary, desperate cherishing. But with him at least the poodle would be assured of a dignified life, a steady stream of affection.

At his feet the poodle looked up at him.

"I should be talking to *you* about this," said the dogwalker. "It's not right, is it? You don't have a say in the matter at all."

No, he did not. Dogs were the martyrs of the human race.

The light turned and the three of them stepped into the crosswalk. Forward. The brightness of the day was upon them . . . he was lucky, he thought, with a sudden soar of hope. Here he was with his two favorite dogs, walking them at a perfect pace for all three. Neatly they jumped up onto the curb. They did not pull him and he did not pull them. Could you go forward forever, with your dogs at your side? What if he just kept going? Across the city, over the bridge, walking perfectly until darkness fell over the country. Sometimes he wished he could gather all the dogs he loved most and walk off the end of the world with them.

When a dog was put to sleep its chin simply dropped

softly onto its paws. It looked up at you with the same trusting eyes it had fixed on you since it was very young.

At the violinist's building he nodded at the doorman. There was a noisy crowd in the elevator, a birthday party of children with conical hats and clownish face paint. He let them cluster and hug the dogs; the dogs licked them.

The attendant opened the penthouse door for him.

"You beat me here," he told her. Usually he did not attempt these minor exchanges, but he was nervous and needed to fill the space.

"Poor Blackie," she said, as he unclipped the leash and hung it. She knelt down and leaned her face against the dog's curly flank. "My husband's allergic to dogs. It's really bad—I mean, he breaks out in rashes, he gets asthma attacks, nothing helps. Otherwise . . . I feel so bad I can't keep Blackie in the family."

The dogwalker stared at her, a realization dawning. It was almost two years now that he had worked for them, and it had never occurred to him that she was the violinist's daughter.

He had assumed she was paid for her services.

"What's wrong?" asked the daughter. "Is something the matter?"

"Oh no," he said, and shook his head. "Nothing. I am going to sleep on it."

This time the elevator was empty. It had mirrors on every wall and he watched the long line of reflections as they descended, he and Sir Henry. In the mirror he saw infinite dogs lie down.

Thomas Edison and Vasil Golakov

IN DISCUSSING THE ABRUPT dismissal of longtime retainer I. Vasil Golakov from his service in the Edison ménage, a number of recent scholars—most notably J. Horslow and T. Rheims, in a paper titled "Edison, Tesla, and Westinghouse: The Queer Undercurrents of Early Electricity"—have proposed that it was a homosexual advance upon Edison on the part of the Bulgarian valet that led to his sudden termination. Lesbian separatist theorist P. Valencia-Sven has taken this bold hypothesis even further, implying that it was Edison's stern denial of his own secret yearning for the strapping Slav that compelled him to expel Golakov from his household.

But the first translation of Golakov's letters from the original Bulgarian, by doctoral candidate L. G. Turo of

Rutgers, sheds a novel light on these fanciful specula-
tions. And although it is indeed likely that Golakov
and Edison had an altercation on the day of the firing,
there is scant evidence to suggest that the businessman-
inventor and his faithful manservant enjoyed anything
other than a purely platonic rapport.

Curiously, as the translation illustrates, the begin-
nings of the rift between master and domestic can be
traced to an elephant execution on Coney Island.

When Edison offered to kill Topsy the elephant, in
1903, he had already lost the so-called war of the cur-
rents. It had been a war of both commerce and science,
and the otherwise successful inventor had lost calami-
tously on both fronts. Having campaigned bitterly to
persuade the public that his direct-current system was
safer than its rival, alternating current—a technology
harnessed by Nikola Tesla and owned by George Westinghouse—Edison was proved wrong by 1896, when
alternating current won the day, and by 1897 he had
sold off the last shares in his old electricity company.

But in the course of the public-relations battle, he
had adopted a perverse strategy: Although opposed to
the death penalty, he had promoted an electric chair that
would use AC to execute convicts and thus showcase

its lethality. And further to defame the rival form of current, he helped an engineer named Harold Brown publicly execute stray dogs, calves and horses with AC—despite his own professed belief in kindness, later to be quoted by animal-rights advocates. "Nonviolence leads to the highest ethics, which is the goal of all evolution," he said. "Until we stop harming all other living beings, we are still savages."

In any case, by 1903 the inventor had long since turned his attention to motion picture technology, then in its infancy. He had patents on some of the first motion picture machines, and when he heard there was an elephant in the area who was slated for execution, he stepped in and suggested a lethal dose of AC. His men would both set up and record the electrocution.

Topsy, the elephant in question, was a disgruntled circus and work animal who had suffered the pains of forced labor, captivity, neglect and abuse. She had responded by killing three men, the last of whom fed her a burning cigarette.

Simple shooting would not have been theatrical enough, for her owners, Thompson & Dundy of Coney Island's Luna Park, had decided to make an example of the rogue. (The execution of animals, an odd extension of a medieval practice, assumes the animal is a moral agent, accountable to the law and therefore punishable in a formal and public context. It is noteworthy that the elephant was not being euthanized or exterminated, as vermin would, but penalized for her sins against God and man by execution qua execution. The ramifications of this apparent subversion, whereby the ultimate punishment—viz., death—also comprises the ultimate elevation/reward, are of course multifold.)

To put a just end to Topsy, therefore, an effective method was sought. Poisoning was tried but failed. Hanging was next considered, then dismissed when the ASPCA objected. (Despite its unpleasantness, to say nothing of sheer difficulty, this method would be used in 1916 in East Tennessee, on a five-ton elephant named Mary.) Finally Edison made his offer, and, ironically, though it was the unsavory nature of AC he would demonstrate with his movie, the ASPCA did not object to the method—perhaps because it was a new technology, and as such must be regarded as superior.

So Edison sent his technicians to the site of the execution and had them engineer and film the condemned animal's fiery death. They attached electrodes to her body, strapped on sandals and set up their camera. The brief filmstrip that resulted still survives, a few grainy, gray seconds. It shows the creature being led, swaying gently, to the place of her doom; there, a white fire rages around her body. She collapses onto her side.

Edison himself was not present at the electrocution. As always, his attentions were claimed by a busy schedule. But according to Golakov, whose letters to a sister in Bulgaria were never mailed and therefore found their way into the boxes of household documents transferred to the Edison archives by the Mina Miller Edison estate, he was deeply fixated on the resulting filmstrip. The valet claimed that Edison—blithe, boastful, pragmatic to a fault and not prone to introspection or idleness—watched the filmstrip privately on a regular basis. He further claimed that Edison often conversed with it, addressing his remarks to the image of the dying elephant.

Here it should be observed that the footage, still extant and now publicly available on various Internet sites, represents an early example of what has since come to be called a "snuff" film—that is, a film that records the willful killing of an unwilling subject. Actual human snuff films have only very rarely come to light, and exist in American culture chiefly as mythic fetish objects, but animal snuff films, whose production is not for the most part illegal, are relatively common.

In Golakov's voluminous letters, a number of the Edison/Topsy monologues are rendered. Most were reportedly delivered late at night or in the small hours of the morning, when the businessman-inventor liked to work; at these times he alone was awake in the house, and during pauses in his labor chose to closet himself in his study with one of his Projecting Kinetoscopes, watching as the blaze rose around the charring elephant's wood and copper-shod feet.

Frequently the monologues concerned matters of business and technology too arcane to be detailed herein: the vicissitudes of carbon filaments and ore extraction, efficiency improvements at the West Orange facility, various properties of nickel hydrate. But often they were deeply personal, and, according to Golakov, Edison must have found in the elephant a faithful listener, at least at first, for his talks began as tranquil ruminations that tapered into silence only when the businessman-inventor nodded off in his leather armchair. As the disquisitions continued over weeks and months, however, they took on an argumentative tone. It seemed the elephant had begun to rebuke the businessman and had even had the temerity to dispute his assertions.

As Golakov presents them, the conversations are of course one-sided, with lengthy pauses into which Golakov believed the burning elephant's rebuttals and queries would have been interposed. A typical excerpt from these enigmatic "exchanges," on the subject of Edison's fear of oral copulation/death, is set forth below.

"I won't do it. Filthy. Anyway, she . . . No, I tell you. No. You women are all the same. Selfish, and can't invent worth a damn. Harlots all . . . That, that wet thing . . . ugh. Like old cow's tongue, or pigs' feet. Disgusting . . . Makes her a slut, Topsy. Wantonness! Nothing less. A wife's duty lies in . . . Do not interrupt me . . . I should have killed you three times if I killed you at all . . . Yes . . . yes . . . I know. I know. I am very sorry . . . I said I was sorry! . . . Is it green? Are there fields? Oh: and is the sun bright?"

Yet Golakov's letters reflect nothing so much as a longing on Edison's part for the approval of the boiling elephant. It is not clear to what degree this imputation is a fiction originating with the domestic, whose mind was almost surely affected by his daily use of the diacetyl-morphine cough remedies then sold widely by Bayer; certainly there have been no corroborating reports of any mental infirmity on Edison's part. But Golakov's documentation of Edison's most intimate personal habits, relationships and opinions bears up well under close scrutiny and does reflect a credible familiarity with the businessman-inventor. Since the inventor had suffered a partial loss of hearing, it is not impossible that he may have welcomed the silence of a celluloid companion. And while almost certainly not accurate in all regards, Golakov's notations clearly have a documentary value in elucidating aspects of the event.

On occasion Edison appears to have conducted philosophical debates with the moving image, defending a rational humanism for which the roasting elephant berated him.

"I am Man. Man has his own destiny! . . . Impractical, I'm afraid. Exhumation and shipping alone . . . I have no time for messing about with your bones, my stubborn pachyderm . . . Commonality? With every breath each of us on this earth inhales a molecule from Caesar's final respiration. And likewise a molecule from

Brutus's breath, as the traitor raised a hand to stab his noble emperor. Does that make us Caesar? Does it make us Brutus? . . . Children, oh, hmm . . . I have several myself; barely remember their names. What? You had none! You trudged under a yoke all the days of your . . . what? False pachyderm! How you lie! Animals do not dream of that which has not transpired. A pachyderm cannot dream of her unborn children . . . Observation, clearly. I am Man; I can see. I have seen for myself how insensate you are. A pachyderm is not given to flights of fancy . . . There is no God in the Church, no: not there. But I begin to see Him. I see Him nonetheless . . . Contradiction? Leave me be. I have work before me."

In the months leading up to the incident that brought about Golakov's dismissal, the conversations he records become increasingly agitated and hyperbolic. Indeed a sort of rageful ecstasy is manifest:

"How you shame me! You torment me with your humility! . . . Murdering pachyderm! I know well what you did. You are no saint! . . . Do not play the victim, my crafty friend. Do not play the innocent! . . . Together, you say? Together! Yes we will!"

At some point, writes Golakov, the elephant evidently became a sort of priestly figure or godhead, despite this antagonistic dynamic. Before her ghostly image, the businessman-inventor would kneel to pray, meditate and ask for absolution.

Edison was still a freethinker then; it was only circa 1920 that the inventor would begin to speak publicly of building machines to communicate with the dead. In his early life the brash businessman openly ridiculed religion and notions of a soul and an afterlife; yet even at the time he had a chronic weakness for magicians and occultists and was an admirer of both Madame Blavatsky and well-known billet reader Bert Reese.

In fact, it was not long at all after his dismissal of Golakov that the businessman would execute an abrupt about-face in terms of his religious leanings— and in the final decade of his life, far from being the out–spoken atheist of his youth, he would ridicule those "fool skeptic[s]" who dared to doubt the existence of God.

Certainly it is true that his second wife Mina, eighteen years his junior, was a staunch Methodist sometimes said to have believed the doctrine of evolution to be the work of Satan the deceiver. But Edison did not always hold the female intellect in high esteem, and he is unlikely to have been swayed by the young woman's pious fundamentalism. It is probable that his newfound faith had its genesis elsewhere.

In any case, it is Golakov's intrusion upon his employer's devotions that seems to have precipitated the termination of his employment. The valet had for some time been pilfering from Edison's personal supply of cocaine toothache drops, which he then used in combination with his heroin cough medicine to produce effects of euphoria and allay anxiety. (He recommended both popular tonics to his sister.) On the occasion in question, a quiet evening in late September, he had ingested both remedies in some quantity, alternating quite neatly between them. As he sat quaffing a nightcap in Edison's closet (the closet featured a slatted door), he had a good view of the scene in the study.

"The giant's stately presence," writes Golakov, "had Mr. Edison transfixed."

He laid himself out on the floor in joyful submission to the flickering vision, and he spoke to her as he always did, but with more emotion. "How you glow, noble beast, in the infinite moment before your own death!"

He rested his forehead on the rug and trembled. "How many times have you died? A thousand times you have died, a thousand and a thousand. I have seen it, like the millions of stars in the sky. And still you speak to me: You hold me in your dead eyes. I know your terrible power." Rising to his feet, hands clasped in supplication, he choked back a sob as he said this, and I began fearing for his sanity. "Yes: yes: yes. You are the Savior. But I see now that you do not forgive me . . . what did you say to me? . . . I hear you. You say: I do not forgive. You say: This is my gift to you: I will never forgive: Now and forever, you are not forgiven."

At this moment, according to the valet, Edison began weeping piteously. In his own state of artificially enhanced excitation, the valet apparently felt compelled to leap out of his hiding place, and, shocked by the sight, the businessman-inventor fell flat on his face, only to recover when his burly valet lifted him off the floor.

What passed between the two thereafter is not indicated in Golakov's reporting. Likely Edison recognized that the valet's volatile disposition and rampant exploitation of substances had become a liability. What is known for certain, from the household accounting records, is that I. Vasil Golakov left the mansion the next day and was never admitted through the Edisonian doors again.

Little is known of the valet after he left the inventor's employ save that his abuse of narcotics continued unabated, for a scullery maid complained to Mrs. Edison twice in the ensuing months that the former assistant was begging for tonics at the servants' entrance to the kitchen.

Golakov's final words on the subject of Edison and his elephant, from the last surviving letter to his sister, clearly suggest it was the drug-addled Balkan, not his employer, who was spiraling into dementia. For after he "leapt out" of the closet to "rescue Edison" from himself, Golakov alleges, the inventor launched into a spirited homily:

He said: "Don't you understand, Golakov? I have seen the future. I have seen in the paradox of her suffering the last end of man . . . yes, she was a murderer, but so are we. And I saw in her eyes the longing of all men for a far better place, for a place where man was no longer cruel and no longer wanted retribution for cruelty; for a place, indeed, where *man was not man at all*. Yes,

Golakov, that was what I beheld: the true and final emancipation of man. For at the end of history man will shed his humanity. Man will be man no more. And this alone will allow him the grace for which he has always longed."

Whether or not there is a grain of truth in the chaff of these epistolary ravings, only Edison could tell us. But certainly one wishes to issue a caution to critics in the mold of Profs. Horslow and Rheims, who, when faced with the evidence of the new translation, may despite it cleave stubbornly to their attribution of homosexuality to the eastern European tippler or indeed the businessman-inventor himself. Should these critics choose to see in the elephant a "symbol" of either heterosexual denial or repressed homosexual identity, they are of course free to do so; and no doubt, in that case, the elephant will have spoken to them as eloquently as she spoke to poor Golakov's Edison, who saw in the dying beast myriad glorious reverberations of his martyred Christ.

Tesla and Wife

I KNEW A GREAT man once. At the same time I knew a great man and a woman who loved him.

When I first met Mr. Tesla he looked like Count Dracula—tall and painfully thin, with cheeks sunken in. It was during the Second World War at the Hotel New Yorker. I was a maid there at the time: my first job out of high school, the first time I paid my own way. He was ancient, his skin as white as his hair.

He had been on the cover of *Time* magazine when he was seventy-five, but later, when I knew him, he was living on scraps from old admirers. For decades he had lived in hotels; it was a suite at the Waldorf for years, but in the New Yorker all he had was a shabby room on the thirty-third floor.

He had invented electricity. Lights, one of the bell-hops told me my first day on the job. Maybe the radio, except Mr. Marconi took the credit. He let companies steal his ideas, said my friend Pia. She was the one who loved him. He should have been very rich, she said, but he was not concerned with money.

He knew important people, and now and then some of them came to visit him. Some were squat men from Europe with square heads and bellies that stuck out; some were American. He told Pia he was inventing a Death Beam. That was why the men from the government came: We were fighting the Germans, and the FBI and the war department wanted the Death Beam.

He kept his pigeons in his room with him. We were allowed in to clean only when his fear of germs grew stronger than his need to be alone. I was glad when he let us in. I didn't want him to live badly. He was strange but very kind, when he remembered to be.

He called the pigeons his best friends. His "most sincere friends," as he said. They came to the window and he fed them, and a lot of them roosted there. He had nesting baskets for them and cages custom-made by carpenters; he had a curtained shower for them to bathe in and casks of his favorite birdseed mixture, rapeseed and hemp and canary. On the floor and on the furniture was the evidence: feathers and white messes. I would go in with my cart and hear birds cooing in the shadows.

He kept a photograph of a pigeon that had died some twenty years before. Sometimes he called her the white pigeon, other times the white dove. In certain languages, he said, they used the same word for both. She was his true love, he said, a white pigeon with gray on her wings . . . later I would read that he had said he loved her as a man loves a woman. He never said that to me, but he did say other things. He said she filled his heart with happiness and that when he'd realized how sick she was, he'd stayed with her, waiting for her to die. When she died a light emanated from her and his eyes hurt from the brightness. He knew then that his work on Earth was ended.

A pigeon might seem serene, he said, but that was a trick of the feathers. The feathers were soft but beneath them it was bloody. That was beauty, said Tesla: the raw veins, the gray-purple meat beneath the down.

I should have died when she died, he went on, but death, I think it slipped by me.

Some people made fun of him for saying he loved the pigeon like a woman, though I never thought it was funny. People love their pets, but the love is tinged with sadness. Because the love is for a pet, they are ashamed of this. They want the love to seem as small as a hobby so no one will have to feel sorry for them. Tesla was not ashamed. He was never ashamed. People did not understand that, and they called him perverted.

Pia loved Tesla like he loved the pigeon.

Since I knew Pia, sometimes I have thought: I would have liked to know that love.

She thought he was as good as a saint—a saint or even more. She had her own problems. One of them was a harelip. Tesla had so much knowledge, she said, that it was as though he were God himself. And like God, he could not pretend he was human. This was why he failed despite all his ideas, why other men lived in comfort with wives to serve their needs and he was alone and poor.

Why God sent His son down to die for our sins, said Pia, was He could not come down Himself. He would not have known how to talk to regular people, she said. Pia was part Catholic and part something else, a religion from her parents' village in Cyprus. I was brought up Methodist and didn't know much about it.

In my church we had God, of course. We also had

God in my church. But He was all downy feathers and none of the dark blood.

How the dust gathered!—on the dark file cabinets, the cupboard, the large safe in the corner and the desk. Tesla forgot the surfaces of things. He didn't need to write down his ideas for inventions, he said, because he could keep them in his head. He did use paper, though; he liked to draw pictures of places he dreamed about. The pages had a few words, as well as drawings, but hardly any math on them. I didn't know much back then, but I had seen an equation or two in high school and I was pretty sure you would need math to invent a Death Beam.

He called me "Mees." He called all the maids that.

Every day he went to feed the pigeons outside the library. He went with duty and an aspect of hope. If he was sick and could not feed the birds, he had a boy do it for him, a boy named Charles who raised racing pigeons. He walked with a cane by the time I met him, because he had been hit by a car two blocks away. His first thought when he got back to his room, with three ribs broken, was that someone had to do the day's feeding for him. He sent out a bellhop with his bag of seed.

Anyone else might have gone to the hospital but Tesla had no truck with doctors.

When I first cleaned his rooms I thought the birds were disgusting. I would avoid the rooms whenever I could and leave them to Pia. She was a harder worker and didn't turn up her nose at anything. But after a while Tesla began to talk to me. He told me how smart some pigeons are, how they see ultraviolet light and remember things for years. He told me homing pigeons were carrying messages for the Army and saving the lives of soldiers, how vast flocks of passenger pigeons had been shot out of the sky for the pleasure of shooting, and five billion had turned to none. He said it was a little boy who shot down the last of the passenger pigeons.

Tesla told me that he chose not to marry. He said love could be all right for working people, and maybe also for poets and artists, but not for inventors like him, who had to use all their passion for invention. He was friends with Mark Twain, who was devoted to his own wife. I think maybe that's why he said writers could get married and still do good work: He didn't want to hurt Mark Twain's feelings.

Pia said he was chaste, and that was why he was not

interested in women. Never once did I see a woman in his suite, except for Pia cleaning. Her husband beat her so badly she went deaf in one ear; her left eyelid drooped from when he flicked it half off with a knife tip.

Women could not tempt Tesla, she said.

One time Pia came in to work after a bad night and Tesla asked if she would go out and feed the pigeons with him. She was limping from a kick to the knee. Marco was handsome and slept with girls he met in bars; sometimes he brought one home and made Pia sleep on the couch while he took the girl into their bedroom. Then Pia would have to listen to them. I was very fond of Pia, but no one would have called her a good-looking woman. Mostly it was the harelip, since otherwise she was fine, warm brown eyes and a nice figure. I think that's why Marco picked her, because he knew she would feel lucky to have a man at all and he figured he needed someone who would work for her keep and would never leave him.

Tesla seemed to believe her stories, how she fell down the stairs, etc. One time she claimed her nose was broken by a children's ball that burst through her kitchen window. I heard her tell him this because we were doing his rooms together. He nodded politely. But I happened to know her kitchen had no windows.

Tesla had close women friends, though none were his girlfriends. He believed women were as smart as men and that one day they would be just as educated and maybe even more so. Back then, in 1943, it was rare to hear anyone say such a thing. He also said that one day people would all carry little telephones in their pockets, telephones without wires.

Anyway, the morning Pia was limping, Tesla invited her to go feed the pigeons with him. She said she couldn't leave work. He said he knew a way she could sneak out if she wanted to meet him in the park. He said, "Please, Mees," and looked at her solemnly.

I was scrubbing the inside of his windows with balled-up newspaper. I said, "Go, go," and promised I would cover for her. Pia never got to walk in the park. At least for me, on my way home to my apartment, I could take my time if it was still daylight, I could wait to get on the bus until the park was behind me, with its cool greenness and its shade in the summer, or its sloping fields of light snow in the winter. Then I dreamed as the bus carried me, dreamed as I was carried along in the warmth above the cold road below. I read cheap novels and I dreamed, but Pia did not know how to read.

She and Tesla went out and were gone for a couple of

hours. I scrubbed hard, tore around trying to do twice as much as I could so that I seemed like two women. It wasn't hard to get fired back then and I didn't want it to happen to Pia.

When they got back she looked happy. At the time I thought it was the fresh air that did it, having the sun on her face when she was almost always inside. I asked her how it had been and she half smiled, which she hardly ever did because it called attention. But she didn't say much.

It was three days later that I knocked on Tesla's door with his new bags of birdseed on a handcart. The different seeds had to be mixed according to his recipe. There was a Do Not Disturb sign hanging on the doorknob, and it had been there too long and was alarming me, so when he didn't come to the door I went in with my key.

He was lying facing the wall, pigeons clucking around him. It was so cold in his room, I could see my breath. A small mourning dove strutted back and forth on his arm and I heard the faint sound of traffic; when he didn't notice the dove walking on him I knew he had gone away.

He had been gone for two days, they said when the doctor left. He was eighty-six, after all, and chest pains had bothered him. Sometimes he fainted. Before I knew it the body had been removed. Later I found out someone made a death mask of his face. But it looked nothing like him.

When I saw him on the bed, nothing but a slight rise on the sheets, I knew I would leave the hotel behind. An idea of a warmly lit house came to me.

We were shut out of his rooms and from the end of the hallway watched government men come and go. They wore trench coats and didn't take off their hats. They carted away practically every piece of paper in all of the rooms. There were policemen with them, standing around in the halls and cracking jokes and smoking. They held the elevator forever and dropped their cigarette butts on the floor, left burns on the carpet where they ground out the burning stubs with their shoes. They took a lot of other things too: the heavy safe, the cabinets and bookshelves and every stick of furniture. When we went in later to clean the rooms they were completely bare. Only a few downy puffs in the corners, and long gray droppings down the walls where the cabinets had stood. The wallpaper had to be stripped.

The mayor read a eulogy over the radio, and people came from all over to attend the funeral at St. John the

Divine. Over two thousand of them, we heard. Even Mrs. Roosevelt sent a condolence note. Pia and I wanted to go but we couldn't get off work; she said a prayer and lit a votive candle.

But I think, even then, that she had left it behind. By *it* I mean the regular world—the Hotel New Yorker and me. She had already gone; she had gone after Tesla. She had no use for a world without him.

And the next time I saw her she was in jail. I went to visit her after she was sent up the river.

She told me the poisoning had been painful and she was sorry for that. She hadn't wanted Marco to suffer, she said, because suffering wouldn't have changed him. But all they had in the house was strychnine, to kill the rats that shared the basement with them.

I was so used to getting along with her that I really wanted to nod, to say *What can you do?* To say that we were still friends. But my mouth was shut. I was almost struck dumb.

When she got home from work the night of Tesla's funeral, she told me, Marco was in their apartment, a dingy basement in a tenement on the Lower East Side. It was a ten-by-ten living room with a grated window at ground level, a sofa and a table; the bedroom was the size of their bed, and the bathroom was the size of a closet. Marco was drinking and listening to music and getting all revved up to go out and meet women, as he did every Thursday and Fridays too. Saturdays he went to see his old mother in Hoboken, who was still bitter that he'd married a harelip when he could have had anyone.

He yelled at Pia as soon as she stepped over the threshold, because his favorite dress shirt was wrinkled. He threw it at her to iron.

She was glad to iron the shirt, she told me. She had always liked the peace that came with ironing. It was a night like any other night in the routine, but for her it was entirely different. Because Tesla was gone and she was thinking of Tesla and how much she had loved him. She ironed and she remembered: dear Tesla with his gentle voice. She recalled his predictions and smiled to think of them, a world where such predictions came true.

By now the shirt looked perfect. Tesla, it seemed to her, believed in the goodness of everyone. Still, they took all he had from him. They took things only he could give and ran away with them.

And then there was Marco.

She kept on ironing and smiling. At last a flatter shirt had never been.

Marco's music was floating in from the radio in the bedroom—Tommy Dorsey, she said. Marco was shaving at the bathroom sink; they used straight razors then. She hung the shirt on a padded hanger and tapped some rat poison into his drink. Then she took the drink into the bathroom to him.

Nothing was ever, ever so easy, she told me. As easy as falling.

She looked so calm she reminded me of the small picture of the Virgin glued into her locker, except with a harelip. She'd thought he would die right there, she said, and she would have to watch it, but the poison took longer than she expected. She thought it would be instant but he was out the door not two minutes after she gave it to him, his hair slick with pomade, taking all the money from her paycheck. They told her later that he fell down in a crowded subway car, at the feet of two older ladies from Brooklyn, where he jerked and wriggled until the car was stopped at a station and they loaded him onto a stretcher. When the police came to her door it was only to give her the bad news, she said, but she nodded and went with them right away. She put on her coat, picked up her handbag and walked right over to the morgue and then back to the precinct building.

"Why did you tell?" I asked. "You might have gotten away with it."

I was sad it had come to this. Not for Marco—the one time I'd met him I'd known he was a vicious kind of person who more or less deserved for bad things to happen to him—but for her. I wished she could have just divorced him, a thing that went against her beliefs even more than murder. Because she wouldn't get out of Sing Sing anytime soon, I was thinking. She would be an old woman by then.

"It didn't matter," she said. "I already saw the dove."

I was looking at the groove in her upper lip and thinking how she was a better worker than I was. She worked without stopping and she always did exactly what they told her. If someone told her to wash the same wall six times, she would do it. Myself I would often stop cleaning and stare into the air, pretend I was floating in a cool lake or flying.

"The white dove?" I asked her. I figured she had pretty much gone crazy.

She said yes.

"I thought the white dove was dead," I said in what I hoped was a gentle way.

"She was," said Pia.

"Oh," I said, and nodded.

"We were there on the steps," she said, "with all of those birds. And in between them was the space where she wasn't. Mr. Tesla showed me. 'This was where she was once,' he said. The third step from the top, I think. We just stood there and threw down the seeds. But I looked at the space. That was when I saw it."

She grabbed my hands and pressed them. She was shaking, she was that agitated, and her hands were warm and damp.

"When Jesus died for our sins," she whispered, "he turned into the universe." She was hurrying to get the words out, as if she feared someone might come in and stop her from speaking. It all came out in a rush.

A minute later the guard came over and made us separate our hands. No touching was allowed. But by then I was almost relieved.

I never found out what happened to her in the end. I know she got an infection from some kind of internal injury; there had been rioting in the prison before she got there and it was still pretty rough. They beat her up worse than Marco had. She wrote and told me she was sick, and I sent a letter to her but it came back to me. By then I wasn't cleaning anymore. I had saved my money for secretarial school and worked as a waitress in the evenings. I slept the rest of my hours away and had no time for friends, absent or otherwise. I thought of the house I would live in one day, with its flower garden and light shining forth from small golden windows.

The prison said she had been transferred, but the second prison had lost track of her too, as though she had never been there.

For me she did not disappear. I had her words and I could never shake them; I had her love for Tesla and his love for the bird.

My own love, it has seemed to me, has only ever been a love of feathers. However hard it tries, it never gets beneath.

She told me Jesus was the world. The sun was God's eye, she said, the oceans were the water of his body, the rivers were the veins carrying his blood. Did I know that? The grasses of the field were his hair and the trees were his lungs, the doves and the birds and the animals were wishes of his heart. Each one a piece of his longing. The blood had run out of Jesus's wounds, she said, and never stopped running. It ran into the oceans, over which the sun set.

All of this was Jesus and was God.

So did I see what that meant? Dead and alive were the same thing, she said. Dead and alive, they were exactly the same.

Love in Infant Monkeys

HARRY HARLOW HAD A general hypothesis: Mothers are useful, in scientific terms. They have an intrinsic value, even beyond their breast milk. Call it their company.

In this hypothesis he was bucking a trend in American psychology. For decades experts on parenting had been advising mothers to show their children as little affection as possible. Too much affection was coddling, and coddling weakened a child. "When you are tempted to pet your child," said a president of the American Psychological Association in a speech, "remember that mother love is a dangerous instrument." This school of thought ran counter to what was believed by those not indebted for their child-rearing strategies to a rigorously monitored testing process. But it was dominant in the scholarship. To refute it, Harlow decided, the value of love would have to be demonstrated in a controlled experimental setting.

He worked long hours, seldom leaving his laboratory. With his experiments he made a name for himself, appearing on television programs and traveling the country on speaking engagements. He was seen as a rebel and an iconoclast. He spoke boldly of mother love, calling it "contact comfort." He stressed its value to emotional health.

But he spoke harshly of his test subjects. "The only thing I care about is whether a monkey will turn out a property I can publish," he said. "I don't have any love for them. I never have. How could you love a monkey?"

To know how love works, a scientist must study its absence. This is simple scientific method; Harry admitted it. The suffering of lesser beings is often the price of knowledge. As he put it, "If my work will save only one million human children, I can't get overly concerned about ten monkeys."

Others were doing bold animal experiments at the same time, in the fifties, when Harry started, and after. Rats were dropped in boiling water, cats pinned down for months until their legs withered, dogs irradiated until their skin crisped, monkeys shot in the heads and stomachs or immobilized to have their spinal cords severed. When it came to the treatment of research animals, Harry was squarely in the mainstream. Only his willingness to speak bluntly was avant-garde.

He gathered disciples around him, young women and men who would continue his work, and decades later he would still be revered by psychology. While acknowledging the problem of what some might call animal cruelty, later scholars would view his collateral damage as a necessary unpleasantness. His chief biographer, a woman journalist, described him as a rose in a cornfield.

He was a high-functioning alcoholic, and there were long periods in his life when he was rarely sober. He had wives—first one, then another, then the first one again. He had two sets of children he never saw.

Harry Frederick Harlow had been born Harry Frederick Israel. Around the time of his doctoral dissertation he had changed his last name, not because he was Jewish—for he was not, in fact, Jewish—but because the name Israel sounded Jewish, and this made it hard to secure a good job. He did not dislike Jews; indeed, he admired them for their intelligence and their education. But others in academia had certain prejudices. A famous professor who was also his first mentor did not wish him to continue to be mistaken for a Jew, so Harry deferred to him.

It was a minor accommodation.

One way to prove the hypothesis was to take a newborn monkey away from its mother and never give it back. Put it in a bare box, observe it. Anxiety first, shown in trembling and shaking; then come the screams. Watch it huddle, small limbs clutching. Make careful notations. Next, construct a wire mannequin that holds a milk bottle. See if the baby thinks the mannequin is its mother. When it does not think so, give it a mannequin draped with terry cloth, but no milk. See it cling to this milkless cloth mannequin.

Repeat experiment with numerous infants. Make notations.

Second, place infant monkeys in isolation, with neither monkey nor human contact save the sight of the researchers' hands entering the box to change bedding or food. Leave them there for thirty days. Make careful notations. When the infants are removed, watch two among them starve themselves till they expire. Notations. Repeat with longer isolation periods. First six months, then a year. If necessary, force-feed upon removal from box. Observe: If left in boxes for twelve months, infants will no longer move. Only life signs: pulse and respiration. Upon removal from box, such damaged infants may have to be reisolated for the duration of their short lives. Notations.

Third, attempt to breed the isolate monkeys to produce needed new experimental subjects. When the monkeys show no inclination to mate, inseminate the females. Observe the birth of infants. Observe that the longest-isolated mothers kill infants by chewing off fingers and toes or crushing heads with their teeth. Notations.

Fourth, create bad-mother surrogates: mothers with spikes, mothers that blast cold wind. Put baby monkeys on them. Observe: Time after time, baby monkeys return. Bad mother is better than none.

Only 8:00 pm, and he was already slurring. He would swing by that party. What the hell. Suomi had said he'd be there.

But first, check the experiments.

Walking along the row of vertical chambers, he gave cursory glances inside—one, two, three subjects in a row had given up trying to climb out of their wells of isolation. The pits were designed, of course, to make it impossible to escape.

One subject scrambled and fell back, a weak young female. She looked up with her great round black eyes. Blink blink. She was afraid, but still plucky. Still game to try to get out, change her situation. The others were abject at the bottom of their separate holes, knew by now they could never climb the sides of the wells. As far as they knew, they were in there for good. Plucky got you nowhere if you were a lab monkey.

Then the boxes where Bill had dosed the subjects with reserpine. These monkeys, too, huddled unmoving. Serotonin had been suppressed; this seemed to equate almost uniformly with complete listlessness, complete passivity. Might be other factors, but still: very interesting.

Back past the so-called pits of despair, where the young female—what had they named her? Minestrone?—was still trying to climb the walls and falling repeatedly. She squeaked at him. Well, not at him, technically. She did not know he was there; she could not see him. She could see no one. She was alone.

Harlow got in the car. Drove. Wasn't far. Hated faculty parties, hardly ever went to them: frivolous. Took him away from his work.

He said this to a new female grad student who met him on the walkway, exclaiming at his presence. She had long curly hair and wore no brassiere.

"Dr. Harlow! I can't believe you actually made it!"

"Work allatime," he said, nodding and shrugging at once. Not as easy as he'd thought it would be. Pulled it together, though. "Lucky. Always have smart wives to help me with it."

She shot him a look of pity: Everyone knew the second smart wife was on her cancer deathbed.

"Some of the faculty," he went on, "these guys don't even work on Sundays. Not serious."

She was looking at him like he was a baby bird fallen from its nest. The free-love ones were maternal. Always acting like everyone's little mommy.

Save it up for the kiddies, he thought. Wasted on me.

These days, Peggy dying like this, maybe he should take a break more often—the depression, for one thing. Felt like the top of his head was weighing him down. Headaches constantly. Chest squashed and nervous stomach. Nothing compared to the chemo, but still. Hair and skin greasy. Plus he was tired, face ached with it. Didn't know if he could have kept his head up if he'd stayed at his desk. Fell asleep with a cigarette in his mouth last night, woke up with a stack of papers smoldering. Something smelled wrong. Burned his eyebrow half off, it turned out.

He patted his pocket for his cigarettes. Full pack. His students were going to be here. Chance to talk to Steve again about the chambers. Steve had said not to call them *dungeons*. Bad for public opinion.

Bullshit, but Steve was good at that side of it. Spade a spade, goddammit.

Saw a garden hose sticking out of a spigot against the side of the house. Turned it on, with some difficulty. Wrestled with the hose till cool water sputtered into his mouth. Cleared his head. Tongue felt less mealy. He wiggled the tongue around in his mouth. Testing it.

"Harry!—I can't believe this—Harry!"

Fat woman from the department, what did she do? Personnel? Payroll? Lumbering.

"Ha, ha," he said, dropping the hose, stepping up onto the stoop and lurching into the doorjamb.

"So you're finally out of your cave! Look who's here! It's *Harry*! Can you guys believe this? Come on in!"

There was the good-looking girl from East Germany who was interested in the nuclear-family experiments, smoking in the corner with Jim. Poor Jim, that plagiarism thing with Peggy. Unfair. But nothing he could do about it. Couldn't get in the middle. He shrugged, itchy.

The jacket: How long had he been wearing it? Felt oily. Maybe it was the shirt. Was it supposed to be white? He could not remember. Gray, beige or white? What color was the shirt to begin with?

"Get you a highball, Harry?"

It was a hard-to-breathe night. Humid, filmy. He squinted. Barely see the kids in the corner, but all of them seemed to be looking at him.

The fat payroll said something about gin. He nodded. Headache getting worse. Bands of light spanning his field of vision.

"Harry," said a guy from the right. "Harry Harlow, right? Hey, I read 'Love in Infant Monkeys.' Great paper."

"Huh," grunted Harry. "Seen Suomi?"

"Steve's not here yet," said the guy, either frowning or leering. No idea who it was. Might be the chancellor, for all he knew. Wished he would disappear.

"Huh," Harry muttered. Guy was already veering toward something out the side door, where a fountain was playing. A twinkle of water? Mermaids?

"Lie down a little," he told the payroll woman, hovering with a heavy tumbler. He accepted it gratefully, drank it down and gave it right back. Good to be prompt. Aftertaste was hinky. "Spare daybed, maybe? Dark room? Cot thing?"

"Certainly," said the woman. "There, there. You poor dear." She leaned close and whispered with obscene intimacy: "How's she *doing*?"

Wasn't a baby bird, for Chrissake. No broken wing. Piece of his mind; tell her straight she resembled a water buffalo. Should be roaming the Serengeti with her quadruped friends. "Holding up, holding up," he mumbled. "Brave girl, Peggy." Hadn't seen her for more than five minutes since what, Tuesday? Busy. She knew; she understood perfectly.

He persevered to the room at the back. Secluded. The water buffalo showed him in. Closed the door in her face. "No buffalos," he said, quietly but firmly.

He fell down on the bed and felt a brief satisfaction.

When he woke, the party was over. Brimming ashtrays everywhere. Skinny kid fast asleep on the couch, legs straight, sneakers splayed on the sofa arm. He stood over the kitchen sink, full of squeezed-out lemon halves and olives. He splashed water on his face and gargled out of a used glass. Didn't see a clean one. Who cared. His mouth was pure alcohol, would neutralize the germs. Made his way out of the bungalow, thirsty as hell. Needed something real to drink.

White light; he blinked on the stoop. It was early morning. Sunday? Legs felt heavy, but he would go to the lab. Still had a faint headache, but bearable now.

Lab was empty. Students must be sitting on their asses this weekend. Pure mediocrity.

Walking the gauntlet of the pits of despair he glanced into Minestrone's setup. Saw the top of her head. She was just sitting there. He kept watching; she did not move. Not a spark animated the creature. Finally given up. Now broken. Her spindly arms hung loose from the sockets, doing nothing. Hunched little figure, staring. Nothing there. It had gone.

Had a flask in a special file cabinet. Headed for it. Deep swig.

In the nightmare, which he'd had in other forms before, he stood beside his beautiful boxes, the boxes of his own design, the boxes that B. F. Skinner himself had admired. He mistook each infant monkey for a beloved soul. In that way the nightmare was confusing. He saw each infant in the heart of its mother, precious, unique, held so close because the mother was willing to die for it. The mother, in the dream, knew what he was doing as he took the infant from her. She was fully aware of what was happening to her and her baby. It was as though she were being forced to watch the infant waste away, left alone in the box—not for the length of its life, perhaps, but for the length of its self, until the self flew out and was forever gone.

In the nightmare it was always the mother monkey he faced, not the infants. The mother, with her wild, desperate eyes. He felt what he could think of only as her passion, like a heat emanating. The mother was crazy with love, mad with a singular devotion. All she wanted was the safety of her infant. She would chew off her feet for it. She would do anything.

But she was trapped, simply trapped. He had put her in a cage, and the cage was too strong for her. When he took the baby from her arms, her panic rose so high it could rise no higher; if she knew how to beg she would beg till the end of the world, scream until her throat split. *Give me my baby back.*

He knew the feeling of loss that would last till she died. He knew it the way he knew a distant country. They had their own customs there.

Chomsky, Rodents

IT WAS ON CAPE COD, in the dump near our summer place, that my husband met Noam Chomsky.

We knew the Chomskys had a house in Wellfleet. The town boasted an impressive roster of leftist intellects. At a pretentious but greasy restaurant we'd seen the dapper Howard Zinn raising his wine glass amid a cluster of ethnically diverse guests. And one weekday night, a bit reluctantly, I went to hear Robert Jay Lifton talk about war atrocities at the public library.

But Chomsky was the only one either of us ever saw at the dump.

In Wellfleet the town dump is practically a local haunt. Because there's no trash collection in town, most everyone drives to the dump once a week. You pay for a square sticker to put on your windshield, pull into the dirt lot past a guard in a tollbooth and make the rounds, distributing the various parts of your refuse load at different sites according to their nature. A few yards away from the main pit for household garbage sits a small shack full of items that occupy the nebulous space between utility and trash; always it boasts a surfeit of drinking mugs and dusty saucers. There are half-broken, bright plastic toys, chipped portable fans and sun-faded life jackets spotted with mold (my husband, K., snaps these up like they're bullion). Chomsky was there with a little girl K. said was probably a granddaughter—she was about the right age, at least, and hovered by his side in the way that indicates some proprietary connection.

K. first noticed Chomsky standing at the open door of the junk shed, holding up a weird object composed of interlocking tubes and chambers in a smoky yellow plastic. It took him a couple of sideways glances to be sure, because the last time he'd seen the eminent scholar on video he'd been twenty years younger. Chomsky was trying to find a taker for the large yellow object, which turned out to be a deluxe gerbil condo.

A tall, affable grandfather with gray hair and glasses— he was almost eighty by then—he was presenting the gerbil condo, K. said, with a kind of desperate eagerness to the assembled company, which consisted of my husband, a couple of indifferent teenagers and a cranky old woman who scavenged the dump frequently. Chomsky did not want the gerbil condo to get lost in the dusty saucers and half-broken toys. You could tell, said K., he thought it was a truly good thing, serviceable and worthy.

The cranky old woman drew near, her shrewish face calculating. Did the object have value? She reached out a hand and tapped the bottom as Chomsky held it up. "Good for gerbils and hamsters both," said Chomsky. "Even mice. Modular and pretty easy to clean."

The old woman made a sour expression and turned away, muttering about rats.

But Chomsky had not been interested in her patronage anyway, said K. Indeed he had seemed to dismiss her on sight as a less-than-serious prospect. He wanted someone who would appreciate the glorious condo for what it was; he wanted to secure the good opinion of a rational person like him, a person with discrimination and high standards.

K. thought maybe the gerbil or hamster had belonged to the grandchild, and was recently deceased. Was this why Chomsky hesitated to just leave the cage there with the rest of the castoffs? Maybe it was the little girl's feelings he was trying to protect.

K. himself had no use for the condo, possessing no rodent pets, but he stepped up and pretended to inspect a segment of tubing.

"Oh. Are you Noam Chomsky?" he asked after a minute, as though this were purely an afterthought.

"Yes, yes I am," said Chomsky, and then returned to showcasing the condo. "Good ventilation—see? And these chambers are for bedding and eating. You put aspen shavings in there. And here's where you hang the water bottle. The whole assemblage, of course, approximates the animal's natural environment. Burrows, et cetera."

"We had a gerbil," volunteered the little girl.

"Mongolian," elaborated Chomsky.

"First we had two, but one died," said the little girl.

"I see," said K.

"Hamsters—now, if you want to get a hamster, those are good-looking but purely solitary," said Chomsky, and lowered his voice. "Strictly one to a cage. Or they'll rip each other's throats out. But your Mongolians are social."

"My brother had a hamster," said the little girl.

"Golden," concurred Chomsky, nodding. "Your basic

Syrian. Most domesticated Goldens are bred down from a single female in Aleppo. In the nineteen-thirties, I believe. 'Course, they were originally exported as research subjects."

"That hamster choked," said the little girl solemnly to K. "It choked right to death. On a piece of popcorn. My dad buried it."

"Hamsters," said K. "Are those the ones where the males have the prominent . . . ?"

"I recommend the gerbils," said Chomsky. K. could tell he was trying to project his voice toward the teenagers, who were holding up a black-and-orange, flame-detailed skateboard (no wheels). He wanted to break it to Chomsky: They were way past gerbils.

"I'd like to take you up on it," said K. "But my family travels a lot."

"They do need care and attention," said Chomsky, a bit punitively.

"You have to clean out the cage all the time or it stinks," said the girl.

"Also," said K., "an animal stuck in a box all its life, I'm not sure I'd feel great about that."

"The Mongolians seem to do well enough," said Chomsky.

"Herky liked to go out. One time I let him run around and he fell in the garbage can," said the little girl.

"Herky?" asked K.

"It was short for Hercules."

"He had no problem making it out of the garbage can then, I guess."

"I had to pour all the garbage onto the kitchen floor."

A harassed-looking mother with lank hair appeared in the doorway behind Chomsky, a sleepy, bobble-headed infant strapped to her chest in a padded carrier.

"Can I get through, please?" she asked tersely, in the two seconds before Chomsky noticed. He stepped back, looking past her to the outside and holding high the yellow condo.

"I've got a great gerbil house! Up for grabs!"

The harried mother, unimpressed, pushed by him and let the door slam behind her, heading purposefully for a pile of used baby objects. K. wanted to tell her, "Hey! This is Noam Chomsky here! The last American dissident!"

"They don't make 'em like this anymore," said Chomsky, half to himself. "This is from the seventies."

"You could always sell it on eBay," said K., and grinned. "You might say, 'Official Noam Chomsky–Owned Habitrail.' It could go for hundreds. If not thousands."

"Damn it," said the harried mother, and turned back to them. There was yellow-white vomit all down her blue carrier, burbling from the infant's mouth in a continuous stream. "Damn it, damn it, *damn* it!" She struggled to pull a packet of baby wipes out of a shoulder bag, and as she twisted to reach the wipes vomit dribbled off the baby's chin and onto the floor.

"Thing barfed. Grotesque," said one of the teenagers, holding the skateboard. He wriggled behind Chomsky, then kicked the door open on his way out. The other boy followed.

"I can't—I can't—" said the mother, and K. saw she was on the verge of tears.

"Here, let me," he said, and held open her bag while she rummaged around inside it.

"You just get . . . so *tired*," she said, shaking her head as she plucked at the baby wipes. They clung together stubbornly until K. helped her separate one from the mass.

"I know," said K. "I have a toddler myself."

"But you're not the *mother*," said the mother, wiping at the baby's chin.

Chomsky had handed the gerbil condo to his granddaughter, who held it precariously as he cleared a place for it on a shelf.

"It shouldn't be on the floor," he said. "Could get stepped on. Or overlooked."

"Could I have another?" said the mother, looking around for a trash can for the used tissue. Finally she pulled out a Ziploc bag full of cookie crumbs and stuffed the used tissue in. Distracted, K. watched Chomsky set the condo up on the shelf, turning it this way and that—possibly to show it off to its best advantage.

"There you go," said K.

"My husband, I mean, he's a loving father, but he doesn't basically *always* have the *responsibility*. From when you wake up in the morning till you—feel better, sweetie?—fall into bed at night. Even when you're sleeping. I mean, you dream about it: bad things happening to the baby. The tension of that—you know, protectiveness never leaves you. Not completely. Everything you have to . . . planning, organizing, knowing every second . . . I mean, just making sure I don't even go to the damn dump without a full complement of *baby wipes*, for Chrissake. You can't even walk out the door without . . . there you go, sweetie. All cleaned up."

K. was nodding with what he hoped looked like empathy, but she barely noticed him. K. had the feeling she was talking more to Chomsky than to him.

"I mean, fathers essentially go on doing what they've always done. Just maybe a little less of it. But the woman, all of a sudden, has to come second *to herself*. Not in theory—because I know my husband would do anything for the baby, in an emergency or whatever—but in practice. Every day. Every hour."

"There are rewards, though, aren't there?" asked Chomsky with a paternal air. He extended a forefinger to the baby, which grabbed it.

The mother was wiping her own hands now, up and down the fingers. K. looked at the baby's face: It was a pumpkinhead, he would tell me later.

K. believed that almost all babies not his own were just a little ugly. He tended to feel sorry for them in their homeliness. But then, whenever he looked back at pictures of our two-year-old when she was six months old or a year, he was shocked at her own over-size melon, fat cheeks and baldness. "I didn't realize she used to look like *that*," he would say regretfully, shaking his head.

"Of course there are rewards, or we would just kill ourselves," said the mother. "That is *so* not the point."

"The possibility exists," said Chomsky, gently unwrapping his finger from the baby's pudgy grip, "that you don't actually *have* to be quite as vigilant as you *are*. Mothers, that is."

"That's what I think," said K. "My wife is tense all the time about our daughter getting hurt. It's this constant anxiety."

"You don't get it," said the mother. "Neither of you. Trust me."

Chomsky and K. shared a glance, and Chomsky came close to raising an eyebrow. K. told me later it ran through his head: He doesn't *get* it? This is *Noam Chomsky*!

K. found himself wondering idly why Chomsky hadn't won a Nobel. K. himself, who had studied phenomenology in grad school, personally disagreed with Chomsky and his followers when it came to linguistics. But he admired Chomsky for his persistence in politics.

"Can I take this?" asked the little girl, and stood up from a pile in the corner with a cobweb on her shoulder, holding up a heavily pocked dartboard.

"Are there darts along with the board?" asked Chomsky, and went to rummage beside her. "Because it's not much good without them."

"Mom says I can only have the kind of darts with sticky stuff on them," said the little girl. "You know, the balls? Not the sharp ones."

The baby in the carrier began to fuss nervously.

"OK. What did I come for? I can't even remember what I came for," said the mother distractedly, jiggling in place to keep the baby happy. "Oh yeah. There was supposed to be a bouncy chair here. With an animal mobile. Has anyone seen a bouncy chair?"

"It got took," said the old scavenger woman. "Right before you got here. A lady in a Beemer."

"Are you kidding? Vincent said he would keep it for me! I drove all the way from North Truro!"

"Do you have a sticker?" asked the scavenger sharply. Out-of-towners had no dump access.

"Yes, I have a sticker. Not that it's really your business."

The baby suddenly wailed, a gravelly, ragged noise in the closeness of the shed. K., having found a small blowup raft he thought would make a good water toy for our daughter, had moved a few paces away and was inspecting it for leaks.

"I can't believe this," said the mother when the baby quieted. "I can't believe it. We had to go to Hyannis yesterday through an hour and a half of stopped traffic, and I didn't buy a chair *just* because Vincent said it was here. I need that chair. I need it!"

"The kind where you plug it in and it vibrates?"

asked K. "Or the kind where it swings and plays the music?"

"The kind where you hang it from the doorframe."

"Oh yeah," said K.

"Then you can do the dishes. You can go to the bathroom."

"Whatever happened to a simple playpen?" mused Chomsky.

"Could you tell Mom I can have the sharp ones?" asked his granddaughter, tugging at his hand. "I'm old enough. Can you make her give them to me?"

"I can't *make* her do anything," said Chomsky.

"We actually have one of those we don't use, I think," said K. to the harried mother, wanting to help. "My daughter outgrew it. What I don't know is where it ended up."

The little girl was telling Chomsky that the dartboard she had at home was felt, with orange Velcro balls to throw.

"Yeah. Well. Thanks anyway," said the mother to K., beginning to edge toward the door.

"I tell Mom I want real ones," said the little girl. "But all she says is, 'You could take an eye out.' That's all she says."

"God *damn* it," cried the harried mother. One of her bare ankles was jammed into the wire hook of a coat hanger that protruded from a thick jumble underneath a table. She kicked it free awkwardly—the heavy baby leaning sideways, sacklike—and then stumbled, slamming her elbow into a shelf. The gerbil condo fell to the floor.

"Is it broken?" asked the granddaughter quickly.

Chomsky knelt down and lifted it, frowning. K. noticed the mother's ankle was actually nicked, a bright, small jab of blood. The baby cried louder and the mother twisted to look past it to the floor.

"Was it rusted? Just take a look, could you, and tell me if it was rusty," she said to K., almost pleading.

He bent down beside her leg. Several hangers were completely rusted, others not at all.

"I don't think I can tell," he said. "Some of them are, though. Yeah."

"It's broken," announced Chomsky gloomily, and tapped the bottom of the cage. "The structural integrity has been compromised."

"Do I need to get a shot, do you think? Tetanus?"

"For Chrissake, you'll be fine, Melinda," said Chomsky.

K. was shocked. He hadn't realized Chomsky and the harried mother had a previous connection.

"I just gouged myself on a wire, Noam! Jesus! Teddy was up half the night crying and I'm exhausted! Jer's away in the city! Could I have one second of sympathy?"

"I get so tired of the constant state of emergency," said Chomsky. "Everything is a personal *crisis*. A kid spitting up is a crisis. A baby chair that's missing is a major injustice. Frankly, it starts to feels like an exaggeration."

"Oh. I see. So, things like this are never urgent to you?"

"Not really," said Chomsky.

The harried mother, white-lipped, crossed her arms in front of the baby carrier and glared at him.

"For one thing, you're not the one with vomit soaking into your bra, your back aching from a nine-month-old that already weighs twenty pounds and a bloody hole in the side of your foot. So it's easy for you to be perfectly relaxed, isn't it?"

"Crisis is big," said Chomsky. "Crisis is not this trivial, daily *texture* of living."

"Sure. If you're a robot, that is," said the harried mother.

K. had no excuse to be in the shed anymore but couldn't tear himself away. He picked up a china figurine of a pig in a tutu and turned it upside down, pretending to scrutinize a maker's mark.

"What I'm suggesting is that emotion can be channeled in productive directions," said Chomsky.

"That's not emotion you're talking about. That's just opinion."

"Opinion—" started Chomsky, but she interrupted him.

"What you realize when you have a kid, if you're a woman, is we're animals and it's hard to be an animal. It's hard work. It's dirt and danger and bile."

"That *particular* brand of gender essentialism—"

"But what you also realize as a mother is—and I don't think men really get this out of fatherhood, I think maybe they get it in other ways, like if they're having great illicit sex or beating the living shit out of someone—is that it's great to be an animal; it's what the core of life is, to be an animal. Not to be human. I don't mean to be human; I don't mean that at all, Noam. I mean to be a *mammal*."

"Oh, please," said Chomsky. His granddaughter set down the dartboard again, a little disappointed.

"Say what you like," said the mother. A coolness came into her voice and it occurred to K. she had a certain steely quality. "Say what you like about anything you want. I don't care. But consider the possibility that there's something here you can't know. Something here you will *never know*, Noam. Something you will *never know* that would change *everything*."

She pushed the door open and slammed out, leaving the three of them alone in the shed. It was just K., Chomsky and the granddaughter. The old scavenger woman had slipped out unnoticed.

K., standing over a table, had the odd impression that the light filtering through the dirty gray windows had shifted or been subdued—as though an object of enormous weight and strange design had moved silently in front of the sun.

For a second, motionless, he remembered the Hindenburg. Great airships of the past.

Chomsky turned his attention to the gerbil condo.

"See? Right there," he said quietly to the little girl. "It's got this crack all the way across the bottom now, from that corner to this one."

"But the gerbils wouldn't mind," said the little girl. "Would they?"

"They might not," conceded Chomsky. "It would work just as well for them. But the problem is, the *people* would probably mind."

"How come?"

"They won't pick it up," said Chomsky. There was a heaviness to him now, and K. thought he looked older. "They won't even take it now, is the thing. They'll just think it's junk, with a crack across the base like that."

"Oh," said the little girl. She blinked, and again K. thought tears were coming. She shook her head but refused to cry.

"Come on," said Chomsky gently, and shifted the gerbil condo to hold it propped against his side so he could take her hand. "Let's go."

They walked out of the shed, their shoulders, to K., looking stooped. He watched out the window, still clutching the pig ballerina, as the two of them trudged toward the main garbage pit with their burden. When they reached the pit Chomsky stood at the railing for a long moment, holding the gerbil cage with his thin arms outstretched. Finally he let go.

Jimmy Carter's Rabbit

He came to see me at my Atlanta office, after his move back to Plains. It was a slow afternoon and the day's sessions were already over when the Secret Servicemen stepped into my foyer. I wasn't expecting company; my first thought when I opened the door on them—with their clean-cut hair, dark suits and earpieces—was *hearing-impaired Witnesses*.

Then I caught sight of that broad, down-home grin.

Our families went to the same church when we were boys, and we had Bible Study together. He was an avid student, hand always shooting straight up with the answers, while I spent most of the class lobbing spitballs at the back of a fat girl's head. Our interests were different: One of us was strong and popular, the other was bookish, but it was a small town, and even though there were some differences between us we were thrown together often enough. We hung out, playing stickball in the meadow behind the general store, or ran a Cowboys 'n Injuns racket in a rotting tree house. Typically I was a cowboy and Carter was one of the braves. One time, if I remember right, he was a squaw.

Anyway, after some neighborhood unpleasantness my parents moved the family to North Carolina. That happened when I was twelve, and contact between Jimmy and me ended.

Come 1981 I hadn't seen the guy in nearly fifty years.

He wasn't seeking me out in a professional capacity, he told me up front. Of course, if he hadn't said that, the conversation would be privileged. No, he just wanted to get reacquainted. Was there someplace we could settle in for a chat?

We sat out on the roof of my building, which had a couple of chairs and a table. This was back before Carter became a hobbyist vintner, but he already liked his vino; I, too, was a bit of a connoisseur. My heart lifted when he handed me an Échézeaux, and I strode boldly through the glass sliders to my liquor cabinet for a corkscrew and goblets. As I turned from him, I recall a kind of imprint on my visual cortex: a former free-world leader leaning back in a chair behind me, his legs loosely crossed. *President*, I thought. *President* and *waiting*. I'd stayed pretty calm till then, but some kind of delayed shock took me. I got butterfingered and dropped a glass.

Left it there. You don't squat and clean up shards in that situation.

Watching the glittery descent of airplanes in the sky, we cradled our drinks and kicked back. I let the burgundy soak my tongue as Ravi Shankar floated out through an open window; my office was, more's the pity, next to a yoga studio. This was before I moved to my more upscale current location. Meanwhile, in the shared lobby—as I would notice a couple of minutes later on my way to the bathroom—his Secret Service detail was scanning dog-eared copies of *New Age* and *Tantric Frontier*.

I needed a second to settle my nerves. I had known Carter before, certainly, but back then he was just a skinny kid with big teeth, your basic Young Baptist Next Door. Myself, I already had a deep voice. I got to second base with Patty Evans while he was still singing like Tweety Bird. But now he wore a mantle of sorts. I had a good career myself, of course, but his credentials were hard to beat. When I looked at his face, media images clicked through my memory like cards in a shuffling machine. The guy had walked the corridors of power like Caesar or Napoléon, for Chrissake. So I have to admit my legs took on a liquid quality. A great vaulted hallway held them all, these massive, looming figures of men, and here was one of the monoliths in my office. Coming to me for help.

Because no one knocks on a psychologist's door to sell Girl Scout cookies. Carter wanted something.

There was denial there, of course. There always is.

Carter told me he considered talk therapy to be "for folks with real problems." And he purported to be free of these. For Carter matters of the psyche were matters of the spirit, and matters of the spirit found their resolution in the teachings of Jesus. Even when we were boys, Jimmy took his churchgoing to heart. Back then, of course, Baptists were more easygoing and not overly interested in politics.

He eased into the confab with a casual narration of his life post-commander-in-chief. He'd published two memoirs and was looking forward to starting work on a novel. I waited patiently as he yapped about Rosalynn and the kids; I was fairly sure he hadn't sat in the limousine for three hours to offer up the Carter family CV.

"Why I came to see you, Bobby," he offered up when the small talk wound down, "was I'm trying to take a deep look at myself these days. Yesterday and tomorrow. I look back at my life so far and I try to make a moral reckoning. Where have I been, Bob? And where do I want to go?"

"Makes sense," I said, encouraging.

I took the liberty of pouring myself another glass of the burgundy. It was an excellent Échézeaux—a '74, if I recall correctly, which carried a price tag in the triple digits.

"I'm not just looking at recent events, Bob. I'm looking into my character all the way back. And when I remember what we put you through, I feel badly. I truly do."

It was then that my bladder put me on notice. In the cloying bathroom, thick with the sandalwood incense visited upon me by the yoga women, I popped a few codeine-laced Tylenol. My head was aching. Was it the spooks in the waiting room? Or was it Carter himself? I have an action practice: Clients know that with me the past is a springboard, not a quagmire. We don't dwell on the mommies who didn't love us enough. My clients are strictly proactive. I don't often toot my own horn, but I've molded Fortune 500 executives out of acne-pocked office drones.

Important to steer the conversation in a positive direction. Carter wasn't a client, but the same tactics applied.

I left the bathroom with my temples throbbing and was quickly frisked by a Secret Service agent, apparently concerned I might have stowed a firearm in the toilet tank. Outside on the roof I sat down again and had barely picked up my glass when Carter leaned forward earnestly and clasped my arm.

"Keeping quiet and letting the blame fall on your head. Standing by while your family was hounded out of town and your daddy put you away in that place. It was wrong, Bobby. Sinful and wrong."

"I go by Robert these days, Mr. President," I said. I had no use for the rehashing of childhood squabbles; mine is a forward vector. Strength and velocity.

"Robert. Of course. Listen here, Robert. I want to apologize. I've always felt distressed by what happened. I can only imagine what you must feel."

Then it came to me. The end stage of the Carter presidency had been a time of low points, like the hostage crisis and Billygate. Those were the landmarks that showed up in the history books, but there were also the small, linchpin moments that turned the tide and got swept under the rug. I'm talking about what happened with the swamp rabbit. The newspapers called it a killer.

The killer rabbit plowed through the water toward Carter's boat in the spring of 1979. Carter was fishing alone on a pond at the time. Startled, he threatened the thing with his oar, splashing at the water to shoo it away. The vermin grudgingly changed its course. Not much of a story, but when it was leaked Carter was ridiculed for telling tall tales. People didn't believe rabbits could swim, for one thing. But soon a White House photographer showed up with pictures of the scene that backed Carter up, showing a large, light-brown hare, red-eyed and dog-paddling, and Carter splashing the water's surface a few feet from the animal in what looked like a feeble defensive posture.

The upshot: Carter was no longer a liar, but still a clown. Comic-strip spoofs of the episode appeared, one of them starring "Paws," a sharklike rabbit menace.

The president had been unmanned.

It was then that I had an inkling of what was going on. The killer rabbit had brought Carter to me.

" . . . Never thought of you as the town bully myself," he was saying. "You could be, ah, insistent, and you didn't always know your own strength, but heck, Robert, that's par for the—"

"The killer rabbit," I interrupted.

"Pardon me?"

"It's about the killer swamp rabbit," I said. "Isn't it. Why you're here."

Carter shook his head bemusedly, the vaguest hint of a smile playing about his lips. "Robert, I came to talk about *you*. And the wrong we boys did in letting you take the fall for us. In letting you alone be punished."

A diversion. It's hard for any guy to admit to his impotence.

Well, I kept at him. For a while, rather than face up to the lop-eared specter, Carter continued to claim interest in the incident that had led to my parents' leaving Plains. He showed a single-minded determination to divert the conversation from its true purpose. I could see how, in your high-level talks, he could have been a tiger. Still, I cycled back to the rabbit. And finally my subtle handling opened the floodgates.

"Oh, all right. Trivial episode, relatively, but I'll give you the story if you really want it."

It wasn't till after the Reagan inauguration, he said, when he went back to South Georgia, that he really thought about the rabbit incident. He had time, in Reagan's early months, to read the jeering accounts; he had time to reflect that there had been nothing out of the ordinary in his behavior in the fishing boat. He had merely caught sight of an animal in the water and, surprised, jerked an oar in its direction. He'd done it the same way you might swat a fly. His train of thought—moving from the Ayatollah Khomeini to Warren Christopher and standards of cancer care at Sloan-Kettering—had been rudely broken. He realized what the animal was a split second later and lost interest. He had seen swamp rabbits before, mostly in marshes; they took to water readily, to escape from predators.

Two of the four rabbit species in Georgia, he said, swam well; only the cottontails couldn't swim.

For a while, he said, he'd toyed with conspiracy theories. The Reagan strategists, after all, were lean and mean, unlike his own friendly posse of good ol' boys with their antiquated notions of honor and straight shooting. He imagined far-fetched scenarios: James Baker creeping through the foliage with a phalanx of hungry coon dogs, scaring rabbits out of their hollows and chasing them toward the pond; Ed Meese, wearing oversize waders and a filthy baseball cap, pulling up to the waterline in a rickety truck with traps full of long-ears foaming at the mouth.

The thing was, said Carter with lazy good humor, he, unlike the Republicans, had long been a friend to the meek and the undefended. Heck, he had signed the Alaska Lands Act. And yet the rabbit had swum against him!

He laughed awkwardly. Clearly he was masking a wound that still ached. I had no doubt the rabbit had affected his conjugal performance.

I'd already put back a good part of the bottle; Carter had barely sipped. I needed a release valve, since my then-wife was attending twelve-step meetings that seemed to consist of a gaggle of hausfraus who had fastened like limpets to the notion that every man jack was a substance abuser. To hear them tell it, a lone Miller Lite in the hand of a spousal equivalent—I use the term advisedly, as there were several lesbians in the group—was the equivalent of a Scud missile. Though only dimly aware of the words' definitions, Debbie had armed herself to the teeth with jargon culled from these get-togethers. Terms like *codependent* and *enabling* were thickening the air like poison-tipped arrows.

"You wish you'd got it, don't you," I said.

"I'm sorry?"

"The rabbit. Hit your mark, man. Instead of missing."

Carter stared at me with his mouth agape. In that moment, the ex–free-world leader looked like a village idiot.

"Would have read better," I went on. "In the history books. You're afraid your name will bear the stigma of that moment of weakness. Of your symbolic impotence."

"Gosh, I . . ." He trailed off.

The inability to speak at all is, in my line of work, highly significant. I had to press home my advantage.

"I know what you're thinking," I said. In a session I would never say this, of course, but we were old familiars, after all, and I felt myself homing in. "Maybe Reagan wouldn't have won at all. Maybe you'd still be president now. If you'd hit it. Who knows? Maybe the hostages woulda come home in time. Maybe you'd be more successful in other areas, too. If you know what I mean."

The pause lasted a while.

Then:

"Well, Bob," drawled Carter. "Now, you may just be right. But the thing is, I didn't miss. I wasn't trying to hit that poor critter at all."

And just like that, the rabbit faded. Slowly but surely I knew the dark form of the old Mullins cat, strung up and skinned. Only had two and a half legs to begin with, limped around everywhere; that was why we hated it. Pitiful. Thing made you want to weep.

We trapped it in a corner, Al Jr., Travis, me, and J. C. Whose idea had it been to club it to death in the first place?

Not his.

"Listen. It was all of us that did it, Robert," came Carter's voice faintly. The wine made my head heavy; it wanted to loll. "Sure, you did the . . . you know, first hit—but the guys were egging you on. I hope you understand you don't have to bear the burden alone. There was a mob mentality. I mean, the hardness of those times took a toll on us kids. I don't believe it was your fault alone. I really don't. I know we were just children. But I want you to know that I am deeply sorry we did not all step forward to take responsibility. I think how you were punished, and I feel for you. I will always be profoundly repentant for what we boys did."

Carter was playing hard at deflection. He'd brought out the big guns.

"What you may want to do at this point is visualize

the rabbit," I said. My mind was wandering. Al Jr. had said we would end its suffering, put it out of its misery. Strength is the principle, now as it was then. Don't cave, I told myself. Do not fall prey to Carter's feebleness. For a while he had governed the nation, but weakness toppled him in the end. The rolling gait of the cat came to mind, how quickly it could get where it was going on its less than three legs. Old Mullins had pulled it around on a plywood cart with a string, but it didn't need the cart. Even when it had been broadsided by the bat, it had struggled to get up again.

In quiet times, when memory floated, I imagined that little cat had been brave.

Quiet times brought on sentimentality.

I looked at Carter, the smudged glass globe against my fingers. Behind my hand the near-empty bottle was a column of light. Carter himself stretched sideways and ballooned as though in a funhouse mirror . . . it came to me in a wash of smells and color, that scene in the alley.

He hadn't hit it. Not once.

There he was beside me, thin and bulgy-eyed. He shook his head, tried to stop the whole deal. Because it was my idea, I was up to bat first. He had put up his hands to grab the bat from me, fell back when I pushed against his chest and stumbled away as I raised the implement.

Down it went. Down it went.

He had never joined in.

"You need to visualize the rabbit," I said, shoring up my supports. My words were not slurring. I've always held my liquor. "Fix it firmly in your mind. The rabbit is what defeats us in the end, no matter what we do." I saw a leaden pinpoint shrinking inward; I saw dry motes of dust, the gray hours. Then my eyes glanced across Carter. In passing it came to me how sad he looked. My eloquence was moving him. Possibly, just possibly, he would be able to let go.

Back then I was advising clients to use punching bags for aggression, often with images taped to them. It was an innovative therapy and independently pioneered. But Carter was fairly sophisticated, and I felt instinctively it would be better to keep the self-expression abstract.

"So what are you going to do with the rabbit? Now that you have it? It's in your sights, Mr. President. What are you going to do?"

For a time there was another pause, Carter seeming to gaze at me.

Before long he stood. "You know, friend," he said in his gentle voice, "all of Creation is under this blue dome of sky. Maybe someone tossed up that bunny's burrow with a plow blade; maybe it had a litter a coyote got into. There are animals that go mad if you kill off their young. Heck, swamp rabbits live maybe two years, if they're lucky. Reckon that poor fella's bones are somewhere near that pond as we speak, covered up in good old Georgia dirt."

At this point he clapped me on the shoulder. I noticed his glass was still practically full: a good three fingers of the good Échézeaux. Was it going begging?

Something in his bearing was lighter. I understood that he was leaving. He wouldn't need to lean on me again. He'd gotten what he came for.

And, sure enough, he would go on to a resurrection. He would rise from the ashes of a failed presidency to attain the stature of a well-respected elder statesman. It's the job of men like me, behind the scenes, to shape and position; sometimes only a nudge is needed. Meanwhile, the public faces of our strength—our avatars, so to speak—are held up as heroes.

But we know what we do.

I took the presidential hand and held it.

Finally it was withdrawn.

"I appreciate you seeing me," he said warmly. "You let me know if you ever need anything."

With that he turned and stepped away. And did I whisper it, or did it only run silently through me? *Out of its misery.*

As he disappeared through the glass doors I stayed where I was, standing. The afternoon had been intense, and I couldn't risk stumbling. It occurred to me he had a point, partly. I was the fall guy for doing what had to be done. I bore the weight of other men's hesitation.

I saw the fullness of the three fingers then. Carter had left me with something.

The Lady and the Dragon

THERE WAS REJOICING AMONG media watchers when prominent newspaperman Phil Bronstein, then the husband of actress Sharon Stone, was bitten on the foot by a Komodo dragon.

The attack occurred at the Los Angeles Zoo, where the celebrity couple was touring behind the scenes so that Bronstein, reportedly an admirer of fierce carnivores, could get a close view of the ten-foot Indonesian lizard. It happened with lightning speed: Just as Bronstein stepped near the giant reptile to pose for a photo, "Komo" the dragon bit him. Jaws clamped rigidly onto the editor's foot had to be wrenched off; the bite severed tendons and necessitated the surgical reconstruction of his big toe. Still, it was widely regarded as comic, and tabloid reports of the incident belie a barely suppressed delight.

Had Bronstein not been married to Sharon Stone, his misfortune would surely have garnered more sympathy than derision, if far less press. As editor of the *San Francisco Chronicle*, he was successful but hardly a celebrity in his own right. But the joke was a clear one: The man-eating lizard was a perfect proxy for Stone herself.

Bronstein's entry into the cage of the lizard was managed by zookeepers, who recommended the editor remove his shoes, lest Komo mistake them for the white rats that were a staple of his diet. And though the keepers' judgment in allowing the lizard and the barefooted man into such close proximity might have seemed an invitation to litigation, publicly the couple was sanguine about the episode, with Bronstein taking responsibility for his decision to enter the exhibit and joking about the encounter. In television interviews Stone blamed neither the zoo nor the reptile.

In the wake of the media frenzy Komo became a highly popular attraction for zoo visitors. His noble brown head with its dignified throat wattle, his homely yet graceful body and his sleepy eyes endeared him to zoogoers, who fondly recalled his spirited nipping of the rich, assumedly virile Bronstein. In their native islands Komodos are top predators, fast-moving and heavy with a mouthful of deadly bacteria for killing prey. But as an individual, Komo was described by his keepers as "tractable" and "good with people," in an internal zoo memo. He had been seized as evidence in a U.S. Customs case against an endangered species smuggler named Wong, and was residing at the zoo while Wong awaited trial.

Komo seems to have basked in the light of his newfound popularity. Keepers say he had previously lurked in the shadows of a fake log in his cage but now took up a position on a prominent rock, where he remained for hours a day in full view of the crowds, flicking his forked yellow tongue and posing.

There were no further incidents of aggression.

When after several months Komo's popularity finally subsided, he was sent on short-term breeding loan to a zoo in Singapore. There for a while he fell ill and was moved to the zoo infirmary. Once he recovered and his stud duties were done—females with whom he mated produced more than 120 eggs—he was again moved, this time to a facility in Kuala Lumpur, where he was purchased for a private zoo by a flamboyant Indonesian billionaire named Tunku Rajaputra. This is where I entered the story, since I was fresh from Texas A&M and employed, at the time, as a large-animal veterinarian for Rajaputra, whose inherited fortune was based on clove cigarettes and natural rubber. He knew of the lizard's checkered past and was, not incidentally, a die-hard fan of Sharon Stone.

By this time Stone and Bronstein were divorced; the fortysomething movie star had suffered a brain hemorrhage and was appearing in the box-office and critical bomb *Catwoman*. Rajaputra, a short but handsome bisexual who exhibited many of the diagnostic characteristics of narcissistic personality disorder, apparently believed he stood a good chance with the actress—if only he could arrange for a meeting. He brought the lizard to a luxury habitat in his vacation home near Sekongkang, on the island of Sumbawa. Other denizens of the private bestiary included two orangutans, a land tortoise and a tiger shark in a half-million-gallon tank. All the animals were tended by qualified caretakers— I had several colleagues on the estate—and Rajaputra spared no expense.

Komo had been captured by Wong's poachers around

the age of five, when he was still a young lizard prancing around in circles and covered in fecal matter. (This was a ritual dance of appeasement aimed at older dragons, who might otherwise eat their offspring.) In captivity Komo had quickly become accustomed to his zoo diet of rodents, chicks and rabbits and now only rarely rolled in feces, with a halfhearted shrugging motion. But under Rajaputra's regime he was fed live baby goats, which he was encouraged to hunt in a special outdoor yard connected to his indoor enclosure by means of an underground tunnel. He hunted in full view of Rajaputra and guests, who were delighted by the spectacle.

It took him some time to fell a kid, which he would typically not kill directly but mortally injure and leave to die. Businessmen standing at the fence would clap and smile when the bite was delivered and the baby goat sank to its knees, its long-lashed, dark eyes blinking closed tenderly as if for an endless dream. As the applause faded and the businessmen turned back to their cocktails and teenage prostitutes, Komo would retire to a corner to shore up his own strength. Goats could run well, even young ones, and he could summon only short bursts of speed. He was no longer in the first flush of youth, and clearly the goats exhausted him.

Finally he would go back to the moribund goat, tear a chunk of flesh from its exposed belly and feast.

There were pyroclastic rocks in his new enclosure and a shallow pond for swimming. Without knowing it, except by a reassuring familiar feeling, he may have recognized the vegetation of his home island of Flores. There were tamarinds, lontar palms and jujubi trees; in the dry dirt he was able to dig himself a burrow, where he slept during the high heat of the day after basking throughout the morning. He was not lonely, for Komodos are solitary by nature, coming together in groups only to eat carrion. Mating is a brief penetration of the female cloaca by the male hemipenis; couples do not stay close. After laying her eggs, the female usually forgets them.

So Komo was at first, I believe, fairly satisfied with his lodgings on Sumbawa. They were superior to those at the Los Angeles Zoo. The mansion and its gardens were on a hill near the sea; the lizard had a decent view of the western horizon and could even, when the time of year was right, see the sun set in the distance with a green flash.

The situation changed with the arrival of Sharon Stone.

* * *

In a fit of drug-enhanced megalomania following cosmetic surgery for the removal of a small wart on his back, Rajaputra had become convinced that the procurement of Stone as a concubine was the merest of formalities. Confident that the movie star would be pleased to become his chattel, he charged one of his junior secretaries with her summoning and transportation to the compound. This secretary, Suandi, spoke only rudimentary English and was terrified by the prospect of trying to talk to important Hollywood persons over the transpacific telephone lines. Thus, instead of calling, he sent various awkwardly worded emails to Stone's agent, manager and accountant, whose contact details were several weeks in the finding.

As the senior secretary Yang later learned, the agent's assistant deleted Suandi's messages immediately, mistaking them for spam. The manager's assistant moved the messages to a folder marked "Potential Stalkers." The accountant's assistant was admitted to rehab before reading the email. Suandi checked his inbox faithfully each morning in eager hopes of a response from Stone's handlers, but was invariably disappointed; and under constant pressure from Rajaputra, who kept expecting the actress to show up for dinner, he finally broke down and asked for Yang's help.

The Sharon Stone who arrived by small plane shortly before the onset of the monsoon season was, admittedly, a few pounds heavier than Rajaputra would have guessed from her movie appearances. On the other hand, her hair was even blonder; she looked refreshingly young and smooth, as though her very skin were made of freshly molded latex; and she responded with a white, toothy smile to his overtures from the first night onward, joining him in his curiously outdated waterbed after minimal cajoling. She admired his mahogany headboard carved with intertwined pythons.

And she assured him that the discrepancy between her real-life and film physiques was entirely normal and a matter of clever special effects, for no actress, she said—speaking upside down through her outstretched legs in a downward-facing-dog pose—could actually be as thin as the tricks of cinematography made her seem.

She practiced yoga every morning. Rajaputra admired her thigh muscles.

The billionaire's English, learned at a British school in Hong Kong, had an Oxbridge flavor. Despite this he was far from fluent and there were many words he did not know; much American slang went right over his head, and to compound the problem Sharon Stone often spoke far too fast. But it was pleasant to immerse himself in the cascade of words, and what he did not understand in her utterances he glossed over, unwilling to admit there were gaping holes in his vocabulary. For this reason he and Sharon Stone did not always comprehend each other perfectly, but acted as though they did.

And while his assumption was that Sharon Stone had come to stay—and a date for their sumptuous wedding should be set sooner rather than later—the look-alike had in fact been hired by Yang for a period of not more than three weeks while the Las Vegas show she danced in was on hiatus. She was always glad to moonlight as Stone, for playing the part entertained her and the money was often good; in this instance the money had been excellent, the seats first-class, the location exotic, and—an unexpected perk—the guy for once halfway good-looking.

He took her to meet Komo on the second morning but offered no introduction as they walked through the gardens, for he wished it to be a complete surprise.

She had been only vaguely aware of the incident at the Los Angeles Zoo. A strip club and two bachelor parties had engaged her services in the weeks thereafter to do stage send-ups of it. On one memorable occasion she had played a nude Stone in high heels, talking and laughing on her cell phone as her husband (also nude) thrashed back and forth in the background in the grips of what looked like an alligator. All of this was juvenile and none of it made much sense; but then, she had not been hired as a drama critic.

And that was long ago now. She had never seen a Komodo dragon in person—in fact, she had never even seen a picture of one—and while Suandi and Yang had warned her solemnly that she must always remain in character, the sight of Komo came as such a shock that she forgot. He was gobbling a fresh kill; his mouth and jaw were covered in blood. The fawn eviscerated beside him bore a striking resemblance to Bambi. And just as Sharon Stone and Rajaputra loomed over his wall, Komo pulled from Bambi a long string of intestines, holding them in his mouth and shaking them vigorously back and forth to expel the inedible matter within. Blood and feculence spattered onto the dirt.

Rajaputra could hardly have known that a seminal incident of Sharon Stone's childhood, which she later revealed to Yang and me, had involved her father, a meth-addicted salesman who split his time between Reno and Twentynine Palms, disemboweling her mother's yappy

Pomeranian with a broken bread knife. The sight of the fawn and the dragon struck a terrible blow.

"Oh my God!" screamed Sharon Stone, and turned away. "Jesus Christ! Jesus Christ!"

As she collapsed against a pillar sobbing, Rajaputra stood by uselessly, wearing a frozen grimace. Having almost zero capacity for empathy, he was not a born nurturer. Finally a young maid who had been working a few feet away came to lead Sharon Stone to a lawn chair, where she patted and stroked the showgirl's shoulder softly to calm her down.

Komo himself, whose hearing and vision were both poor but whose sense of smell could pick out a dead bird five miles away, went on eating mechanically in a state of some befuddlement, possibly disoriented by the heady scent of Sharon Stone's midpriced perfume.

Rajaputra had believed the lizard would please Sharon Stone, indicating a commitment on his part to her personal heritage. Watching her cry on the lawn chair, however, pretty face in her hands, shoulders and breasts heaving, he was unsure. She was a woman, after all, and women were famously weak in the face of gore and violence. She was divorced now from the Jewish media tycoon whom Komo had so righteously wounded three years before; Rajaputra had thought this would distance her, perhaps even allow her to see in the lizard a kind of cheerful ally against all the Jews; but clearly she was still petrified of the monster.

For her part, Sharon Stone was recovering rapidly. As she hiccupped on the chair she reminded herself this had nothing to do with the deceased Widdle Puff. Her father was also long dead, run over by a tweaking pre-teen at an off-road vehicle rally in the Imperial Dunes. As for the poor little deer, she reflected, well, it was sad. It just was. But she'd tried to be a vegetarian once and it was super boring; plus she'd had venison for the first time this past Thanksgiving. Pretty good. So she wasn't one to talk, as far as eating deers went. And her own dog, a Boston terrier, was safe in the care of an elderly neighbor.

No one was trying to hurt her. She was going to be fine. She had to get back into character and scrub her face of its streaky makeup.

She smiled tearfully at the maid, took a deep breath, rose from the chair and nodded at Rajaputra.

"I'll be fine. Gimme a couple of minutes," she promised.

She sat down on the ground in sukhanasa, folded her fingers into ling mudra and closed her mascara-clotted eyes to prepare for healing. It crossed her mind, before she began clearing it, to wonder if the real Sharon Stone would have yelled out "Jesus Christ! Jesus Christ!" But probably it was OK; the star was rumored to be a Buddhist these days.

The maid curtseyed and retreated.

Meanwhile, Rajaputra came to a decision.

He left Sharon Stone where she was and came looking for me. He would tell me to kill the lizard, kill it immediately, shoot it point-blank through the head. He would have liked to do the deed himself, in full view of his assembled servants, but he suspected Sharon Stone would not appreciate that. If he were a woman, he thought, he would find it highly erotic, but he was not a woman and he was certainly not Sharon Stone. She had already refused a leopard coat he had offered her, on the grounds that it was not nice to flay dead creatures and steal their furry coverings. This was what he had gathered, at least. He did not quite fathom her religion, but no doubt in time he would learn to predict its irrational prohibitions.

Of course, I had come to be fond of Komo and was not inclined toward murder, even beyond the fact that it was illegal and went against the ethics of my profession.

But I had worked for Rajaputra for almost a year by then and knew the billionaire's volatile moods all too well, so I agreed to dispose of the lizard, provided Rajaputra would permit me to use lethal injection instead of a firearm.

Rajaputra contemplated the request for a few seconds, then seemed to realize the gun gesture would work only if he himself were the shooter. I would steal his fire if he let me kill the dragon myself with his favorite .45. Mine would be the glory. Other staff might see the execution and think I was more manly.

"Fine, fine," he said hurriedly. By now he was quite transparently afraid I might in fact cling to the firearm idea, which he himself had foolishly handed to me on a platter. "Yes. Injection. Do it today! And send the skin to Andre in Tokyo. I want a jacket and two pairs of boots. Size 26 men's."

Then he returned to Sharon Stone, who by this time was lying on her back on a towel and pulling up her legs one by one into vatayanasana, the wind-relieving pose.

I ducked into staff quarters to consult with the chief animal keeper, my confidant in matters of herp care. We did the math and decided on an appropriate dose of sedative; we made calls; I filled a syringe; we pulled on our

protective legwear and, along with two assistant keepers, marched over to Komo's indoor enclosure, where the
lizard was by then slumbering. He had consumed about
40 percent of his body weight in a single sitting; seeing
my patient was full of deer, I upped the dosage.

It took Sharon Stone almost a week to realize that her
situation was less than ideal. The revelation came when
Rajaputra presented her with a diamond ring hidden in
a chicken pot pie (he was convinced the pot pie was a
rare American delicacy, but his Japanese chef, annoyed
to be asked to prepare such plebeian fare, had actually
ordered the pies online from Marie Callender's). When
Sharon Stone remarked that the ring was beautiful but
closely resembled a symbol of engagement, Rajaputra
told her she was free to choose whether they married in
four weeks or six. After a brief bark of laughter, Sharon
Stone sobered up; she could see the billionaire was not
joining in her merriment. She told him with regret that
she had obligations back home, to her career, her fans
and above all—remembering in the nick of time a tid-
bit from the tabloids—her adopted son Roan. He was
still a toddler and was staying with his grandmother,
she added quickly, at the moment.

Generously Rajaputra conceded her son Roan could be brought to join them. But perhaps the boy was not necessary? For he would give her many more sons, he said, and better ones too; she might be well into her forties, but his sperm were like superheroes. They could go anywhere and do anything.

"Well, you know," said Sharon Stone distractedly, both amazed and insulted, now that she thought of it, that she was actually being seriously mistaken for a woman in her forties, "he's my son, after all. I do love the kid."

"You may have him, then," said Rajaputra regally.

Sharon Stone wondered what else to say. Until now she had thought the billionaire highly eccentric, true; but she had not worried too much about it, for extreme wealth was well known to distort. The fact that he wore an unsheathed dagger tucked into his trousers at all times, the fact that he allowed no plants, vegetables or fruit to touch his skin and bathed in a solution of iso-propyl alcohol, the fact that he kissed a laminated picture of Roy Orbison every night before bed and liked to pretend to be a mewling infant during sexual inter-course—all these had struck her as essentially harmless. She saw now that she had misjudged.

She felt it best to go along for the moment. There was no point in open conflict. So she smiled and chose late November for the ceremony.

That night she sought out Yang in his office in the east wing of the mansion and begged. He agreed to assist. He had foreseen this possibility. Relief flooded through her, for what if the billionaire's staff had been loyal to him? She threw her arms around Yang and thanked him profusely. She would never forget his kindness.

This was how it came to be that Sharon Stone left the island in the middle of the night, first in a skiff, then in a large power yacht. She was smuggled out of the compound at 3:00 am by Yang and me, guided on foot through the backwoods of the property, the beams of flashlights bouncing around over tree limbs and vines and her Ked-shod feet, mosquitoes stabbing at the back of her neck. Finally we emerged onto a beach, where a few hundred yards from the shore the yacht was anchored, and rowed her out over the reefs in a shallow wooden boat. On the yacht she hugged us and shook our hands again, desperately grateful; she offered us a thick gold necklace Rajaputra had given her, as well as her engagement ring. Yang declined, embarrassed; I broke it to her that the diamond was a CZ.

She smiled sadly at us and promised to drop us an email when she reached home safely. Then she was ushered belowdecks into a dark storage room—a cautionary measure, lest a nearby police boat draw close and demand an inspection, for the authorities were in Rajaputra's pocket.

The room had a porthole but through it nothing was visible save the black of the sky. Sharon Stone could make out no features inside, either, so she sat down on the foam they had laid out for her on the floor and soon curled up and fell asleep.

When she woke in the early hours of the morning she was conscious of a rank smell; it reminded her of the stale body odor caked into the blue floor mats at her yoga gym. Then she sat up and saw the mesh of the cage. Komo was crouched within, his large flattish head only a few feet from her face.

She stifled a cry. The lizard regarded her stoically. After a time he flicked out his tongue. He seemed to be drooling.

Rajaputra had informed her of the lizard's death on the day of its ordering, and she remembered a pang of regret. She had suspected the demise of the animal was her fault, and she had tried to forget it. Yet she was confident this lizard was the same one. Sitting on the foam mattress, feeling a little queasy from the boat's motion, she had time to study it. It wasn't exactly cute, but there was something endearing about the big guy, she wrote me later in an email. He had a certain calmness she liked very much. He was sturdy.

She felt grateful he had not been killed. A sense of euphoria washed over her, for both the lizard and herself. She would never complain again, she told herself, would never measure herself against more successful people. Just living was success enough. She was the luckiest woman in the world.

Presently there was a knock on her door and a sailor entered with a plastic tray of food.

"Is it safe in here with him?" she asked, but the sailor only bowed and nodded. He did not speak English.

She put some of her rice noodles in the cage with the lizard, who looked hungry, but he did not touch them.

"OK," she said, nodding. "I know you're more of a meat guy. I just thought I'd offer."

Later another sailor came in. He looked Indian to Sharon Stone, since he wore a turban. He bowed and smiled, then bustled around the cage, checking the door latches and the lizard's water bowl. But maybe he was not Indian: Did Indonesians also wear turbans sometimes? It was too confusing. And though she felt exuberant in the knowledge of her happy escape, she was still too shy to ask him.

Before this trip she had barely heard of Indonesia, and then last night Yang had told her it was the fourth-biggest country in the world, people-wise. And India was over a billion strong. Along with China, it was about to take over the world, Yang had said, slightly apologetic. In just a few years America would be a minor country, with nothing left of its brief foray into world domination but mountains of plastic and staggering debt. Its national parks and forests would be sold off to richer countries, and what remained of its crumbling cities would be turned into theme parks for foreign tourists. Who knew? She had always thought India was a kind of quaint little place with spicy food, where everyone did yoga and the women drew red spots between their eyes, a shame because otherwise they were pretty. The men had cute accents but bad facial-hair stylings. A good makeup guy could do wonders with the entire country.

"Where is the dragon going? Is he also going to the airport?"

"We're making a special stop for him," said the Indian. "He's being repatriated."

"How long?"

"Just a few hours. Sorry for the discomfort, Mrs."

"Well, shit," said Sharon Stone. "This is nothing. This is great. Try the discomfort of being some crazy freak's sex slave for the rest of your life."

"Of course, Mrs. I get it."

"So thank *you*. All of you. I mean, you guys are, like, my total *saviors*."

"I saw you in *The Muse*," said the Indian, and smiled radiantly. "You were absolutely fantastic!"

"Oh. Thanks, but you know. I'm a ringer."

"Excuse me?"

"I'm not the real Sharon Stone. I look like her, is all."

"Ah! Sure. Sure sure sure."

"No, really!"

"Sure sure. I get it, Mrs. You have my word. Your secret is safe with me."

"But . . ."

"I also liked you in *Catwoman*. Of course, it was not your best film. I will not lie to you, Mrs. Stone. But your performance was exemplary."

"I mean, thanks, but—"

"Do you know Halle Berry? Is she a nice lady?"

Sharon Stone gave up.

"Very nice," she said, and smiled sweetly. A little creative license. "If you can get past the bad breath, that is."

Sharon Stone was allowed to go up on deck when they reached the island. The lizard's cage was difficult to fit through the door of the storeroom, and it took six men to move it. She watched as they lowered the cage on a hook into a large motorboat; at the last minute she asked if she could go with them.

"We're just going to leave this fine fellow on the beach," said the Indian. "This is one of his home islands. Part of a national park just for him and his buddies. It won't be a long trip."

"Still," said Sharon Stone. "I would like to see it. Please?"

"Certainly, Mrs.," said the Indian.

She climbed down the ladder and sat next to him in the boat. The bay they were approaching was undeveloped—nothing but a gently curving sandy beach, deserted, and above it dull dirt-brown hills dotted with a few scrubby trees. She looked at the lizard's hands through the cage, or were they feet? The fingers were kind of fat and wrinkled and the sharp claws gray and dirty. They reminded her of a great-aunt she'd visited in Scarsdale. Mean and crusty. But that wasn't the lizard's fault.

She looked at his face and felt a hole in her stomach at the thought of him being left here.

Gone. She would be alone then, she thought.

The feeling persisted as she watched from the boat: The men heaved the cage onto the sand, opened it, and stood back with forked sticks, waiting for the lizard to emerge. Eventually he did, though he seemed to be in no great hurry. She never took her eyes off the lizard as they lifted the empty cage onto the boat again, as the lizard sat solid and unmoving on the sand, facing them as the boat pulled away. She admired the lizard's posture—even, she thought with a wild puncture of hope, loved it. Her heart beat fast. At once graceful and ugly, humble and pugnacious. She could not explain it to herself, but it was reassuring.

It was this posture, this demeanor, that she would seek out in boyfriends and finally a husband. For the rest of her life she would look for these qualities.

Back on Sumbawa, Rajaputra was told that Sharon Stone had been called away suddenly to tend her sick little son; she planned to return, of course, when the boy was well again, Yang and Suandi told him. Rajaputra nodded sagely and began looking at printouts of pictures from a Britney Spears fansite. Within a few weeks he had forgotten his putative engagement, and Sharon Stone herself was a dim memory.

When a new jacket and two pairs of cowboy boots arrived from Tokyo, made out of what looked a little like snakeskin but was in fact plain old leather, he gave them to a kitchen boy of whom he was seeking favors.

Komo, living a few miles from where he had hatched and climbed his first tree, passed much of his time swimming in the ocean.

Walking Bird

ONE OF THE BIRDS was lame, struggling gamely along the perimeter of the fence. The bird was large, a soft color of blue, and rotund like a pheasant or a hen. Its head was adorned with a crown of hazy blue feathers, which had the curious effect of making it seem at once beautiful and stupid.

A family watched the bird. It was a small family: a mother, a father and a little girl.

The fat blue bird had white tape on one knee and lurched sideways when it stepped down on the hurt limb. The little girl sat on the end of a wooden bench to watch the bird, and the mother and father, tired of walking and glad of the chance for a rest, sat down too.

This was inside the zoo's aviary, an oval garden with high fences and a ceiling of net. Here birds and visitors were allowed to commingle. Black-and-white stilts stood on straw-thin legs in a shallow cement pond and bleeding-heart doves strutted across the pebbly path, looking shot in the chest with their flowers of red.

The little girl watched the lame bird solemnly as it hobbled around the inside of the fence. There was something doggedly persistent in the bird's steady and lopsided gait; it did not stop after one rotation, nor after two. The little girl continued to gaze. At first the mother and the father watched the little girl as she watched the bird, smiling tenderly; then the mother remembered a household problem and asked the father about it. The two began to converse.

The zoo was soon due to close for the day and the aviary was empty except for the family and the birds. Small birds hopped among the branches and squawked. Large birds stayed on the ground and sometimes made a quick dash in one direction, then turned suddenly and dashed back.

A keeper came into the aviary in a grubby baseball cap and clumpy boots. The little girl asked her why the lame bird did not fly instead of walking. The keeper smiled and said it was a kind of bird that walked more than it flew.

"But *can* it fly?" asked the little girl. "Could it fly if it wanted to fly?"

The keeper said it probably could, and then she moved off and did something with a hose. The mother and father talked about flooring.

The little girl got off the bench and followed the lame bird, clucking and bending and trying to attract its attention. It ignored her and continued to walk along the inside of the fence, around and around and around.

The aviary was not large so each circuit was completed quickly. But the bird did not stop and the girl did not stop. After a while the father remembered his life outside the aviary, his office and his car and his stacks of paper. His presence in the aviary became instantly ridiculous to him. He got up from the bench and told the little girl it was time to go. The little girl said no, she was not ready. She wanted to stay with the bird. The father said that was too bad. The little girl tried to bargain. The father became angry and grabbed the little girl's arm. The little girl began to cry and the mother waved the father away.

It was several minutes before the mother could fully comfort the little girl. During this time the father left the aviary and opened his telephone. He paced and talked into the telephone while the mother sat on the bench with the little girl, an arm around her shoulders. He waved to the mother and pointed: He would wait for them in the car.

The mother told the little girl her father loved her very much, only he was busy. He had stress and pressure. He did not mean to frighten her by grabbing. The little girl nodded and sniffed.

When the little girl was no longer agitated, her mother wiped the tears from her face and the little girl looked around. She told her mother she could not see her bird anymore. Her mother put away her tissue and then looked around too. The bird was not visible. Through the leaves in the trees came a glancing of light; the stainless steel dishes were empty. The water in them was still.

The mother looked for large birds on the dirt of the ground and did not see them. She stood and looked for small birds in the green of branches but did not see them either.

"Where is my bird?" asked the little girl.

The mother did not know. She did not see the lame bird and she did not see the other birds. She did not even hear them.

And yet time had barely passed since the birds were all there. The mother had barely looked away from the birds, she thought now. She had attended for only a few minutes to her child's brief and normal misery.

"It's time to go, anyway," said the mother, and looked at her watch. "The zoo is closing."

The little girl said that maybe the birds flew out at night, through the holes in the net, into the rest of the world.

The mother said maybe. Maybe so.

As they left the aviary the little girl was already forgetting the bird. She would never think of the bird again.

There was almost no one left in the zoo, none of the day's visitors. But the visitors the mother did see, making their way to the turnstiles, were all walking with a slight limp, an unevenness. She wondered if they could all be injured, every single one of them debilitated— but surely this was impossible. Unless, the mother thought, the healthy ones had left long ago, and what she now saw were the stragglers who could not help but be slow.

Ahead of her the limping people went out and vanished.

Along the path to the exit, the cages seemed empty to the mother; even the reeds around the duck ponds faded, and the signs with words on them and images of flamingos. The mother looked upward, blinking. In the sky there was nothing but airplanes and the bright sun.

The mother's eyes felt dazzled. The sky and the world were all gleaming a terrible silver. How she loved her daughter. Urgently she took hold of the little girl's hand. She felt a brace of tears close her throat.

Why? It had been a fine day.

| Acknowledgments |

Many thanks to the following for their prior publication of these stories. For "Sexing the Pheasant," *Sonora Review* 53, 2008, as well Heide Hatry and her book *Heads and Tales* (Charta Art Books, 2009). For "Girl and Giraffe," *McSweeney's* Issue 22, 2006. For "Sir Henry," *Famous (Electric Literature)*, Inaugural Issue, 2009. For "Thomas Edison and Vasil Golakov," *SEED Magazine*, 2006, and also *Tin House*, The Fantastic Women Issue, 2007. For "Love in Infant Monkeys," *Willow Springs* 60, 2007. For "Chomsky, Rodents," *The Columbia Journal* Issue 47, 2009. For "The Lady and the Dragon," *Triquarterly* #133, 2009, guest-edited by Donna Seaman. For "Walking Bird," *Fairy Tale Review* Green Issue, 2006, as well as *Long Story Short: Flash Fiction by 65 of North Carolina's Finest Writers*, edited by Marianne Gingher, 2009.

| About the Author |

LYDIA MILLET is the author of six novels, including *My Happy Life* (2003 PEN-USA Award for Fiction) and most recently *How the Dead Dream*, a *Los Angeles Times* Best Book of 2008 and the first in a trilogy about extinction. She lives in the desert outside Tucson, Arizona with her husband and two young children.